Defending Destiny

Molly Daniels

Science Fiction/Time-Travel

Sea Princess Books
First City Books

A Sea Princess Book
Science Fiction/Time Travel
Defending Destiny

Front Cover Design by Mycah Clements
Back Cover Design by Brianna Wilinson
Edited by Leanore Elliott
Proofread by Brian K. Morris

PUBLISHER
Sea Princess Books
First City Books

Dedication:

Big thanks to everyone who helped and supported me on this project! To my family, who tolerated me spending large amounts of time at the computer; various friends who read snippets and told me where to improve; to the readers who read the 'sneak peeks' the past three years and begged me to finish this story; to you, my awesome readers who bought this book.

I'd also like to thank Ron Wise and his graphic arts students at Vincennes University; specifically Mycah Clements and Brianna Wilinson for their beautiful cover art; Leanore Elliott, who took my words and improved them; to the following people, in no particular order: Brian K Morris, Amy Hale, Cathy Jackson, Anny Cook, BC Brown, Jean Joachim, Nancy Riggs, Carol Preflatish, Daniel Newell, Stephen Zimmer, and Holly Phillippe, who have had such an impact on helping me grow as a writer.

Table Of Contents:

Part One:

Defending Andrea

Prologue

"We are here today to celebrate the life of Andrea Turner-Mueller-Sterling-Von Werner." The pastor cleared his throat, glanced at the paper in front of him, and continued. "I had the pleasure of watching Andrea over the years, and she was so full of life, so vibrant, and active in her community…" His voice droned on and on.

Paige Turner-Stanton leaned toward her husband Greg and sniffed. "Andi was certainly 'active' in her community; half the men she screwed are here."

"Quiet." Her twin brother Sage elbowed her in the ribs. "Don't talk about her that way."

"As if you don't know it's true. How many funerals have you been to where the men outnumber the women?"

Warm breath fanned her ear.

"Paige, you're making a scene. Calm down."

"I am not," she hissed, but quieted down.

"Is there anyone else who would like to share their memories?" The minister peered over his half-moon glasses.

Paige wrinkled her nose. "I hope we're not about to hear how Andi was the love of everyone's lives."

"Be nice."

"I would." A somber voice from the back sounded. "Shall I come up there?"

"Please." The pastor looked relieved.

Paige craned her neck, trying to see who had spoken. As the man made his way closer, she frowned, not recognizing him.

The man stepped to the podium and smoothed his blue and gray tie over his khaki shirt. "For those who don't know me, I'm Frank Gillespi, Andrea's manager for the past ten years. When I met her, *'Auuun-dree-ah'*, as she insisted I call her, was, pardon the expression, an immature brat." Frank paused as a collective gasp moved through the crowd. "Hold on, I'm not done. As I was saying, she was impulsive; had her own ideas about how her life should be and fired me five times in the first three days."

Laughter sounded.

"Over the years, she calmed down and accepted my council, and we grew to respect each other. She didn't mind when I reverted to the more natural 'Andrea', and in return, she gave me a raise instead of a pink slip."

More laughter was heard.

Paige crossed her arms. "I suppose he's a stand-up comic in a former life?"

"Who cares? He's livened up the crowd." Greg squeezed her shoulder.

"Anyway, last week we had a meeting and Andrea..." Frank's voice broke. Clearing his throat, he continued, "Andrea told me she wasn't afraid of death, that she'd lived a full life and though the cancer consuming her was taking its toll, she intended to fight it to the end. I was told her final words were 'I'm ready', which I feel embodies her true nature. Andrea was ready for anything. Thank you." His voice cracked on the final word and clearing his throat again, Frank stepped down to return to his seat.

The minister waited a moment before returning to the podium. "Is there anyone else?"

Suddenly, the lights flickered, and a murmuring could be heard. A woman screamed, then another.

"What happened?" Paige turned to look at the crowd, then gasped. "Greg? Greg! Where are you?"

Chapter One

Andrea Von Werner opened her eyes.

"Welcome, Andi. We've been expecting you." A man wearing a white shirt and blue slacks stood by her bed, tapping keys on a computer keypad. "How do you feel?"

"Who are you? Where the hell am I?" She struggled to sit up, but a wave of dizziness engulfed her.

"Relax. What you're feeling is perfectly normal."

Closing her eyes against the vertigo, Andrea lay back down. "Normal? You don't look like God or the devil."

"That's because I'm neither. I wish this aspect of the journey had made it into the history books and religion, but no. Catholics fear us, some religions know, yet believe twisted tales, and Hollywood got it all wrong." He tapped a final key and heaved a sigh. "My name is Joshua and I'm your Transitional Angel."

Andrea blinked. "My what?"

"I'm here to help you transition to your next destination. Some go to Purgatory, Limbo, Waiting

Station, whatever. I help you figure out what you're going to do next."

"I thought I'd die and wake up in either Heaven or one of the rings of Hell."

"That's a huge misconception." He shook his head. "Are you feeling better? Let's help you up."

"I think I can sit up on my own," Andrea snapped. She rolled to her side and pushed herself up on one elbow, wincing at the pain in her legs. "I thought all my pain was supposed to be gone."

Joshua assisted her to a sitting position and arranged the blanket over her legs. "Another misconception. You were in bed how long before you died? You're simply a little *stiff*." He chuckled at the play on words. "That's why Transition is here....to guide you on your way. Are you still feeling dizzy?"

"No." Andrea rotated her arms and flexed her ankles. "How soon can I get on my feet?"

"If you're feeling up to it." Joshua threaded his arm through her left one. "On three. One...two...three. Ooof!" He wheezed as one of her legs refused to cooperate and Andrea fell against him.

"What is wrong with you? I wasn't ready. Help me sit up again." Frustrated, she struggled to a sitting position. "I say when." She gripped Joshua's arm and blew out her breath. "Okay, one...two...*now*." She threw her upper body forward and managed to stand, wobbly at first, but grabbed the dresser until her balance steadied.

"Do you feel up to trying to walk, or do you want to stay in bed?"

Andrea gritted her teeth. "At least help me over to the chair. I'm not going to get better if I stay in bed."

"Okay. You set the pace." Joshua's voice was full of doubt.

Andrea slid her feet forward and managed to shuffle five steps then she collapsed into the wing-backed chair. "What's the standard stay here, anyway?" She looked down as Joshua placed a blanket over her legs. "I thought I'd be in my pink Chanel suit. What the hell did my sister put me in?"

"Another misconception. You don't get to have your burial clothes until you decide where you're going next. Think of this as—"

"I'm stuck in this monstrosity?" Andrea plucked at her blue shirt and loose black slacks. "I've decided to go to Heaven, so I demand you bring me my suit at once."

Joshua pursed his lips as he moved toward the computer terminal and tapped the keys. "That's not quite how this works. You have to meet with your Transitional Counselor first—"

"Transitional what? I thought you were supposed to help me to the next phase of this journey. Who's in charge? I demand to speak to your boss."

"That won't be possible. Raphael is on assignment and Devon is still processing your paperwork. I can certainly let Donatello know you're eager to begin your sessions."

Andrea shifted in her seat. "What sessions? I've decided, so send me on my way."

"Andi, that's—"

"My name is not Andi! It's pronounced Aun-drea. Will you at least get that right?"

"My apologies. Your file may have gotten confused with another 'Andrea'. I will make a note of your preference." Joshua's fingers flew over the keyboard. "Now, if you permit me to finish, you will spend a day or two with me, until you're back on your feet, and understand all procedures. Next, you'll meet with your Transitional Counselor-in your case, Donatello and discuss your options, review your life, and make further choices. Finally, you'll meet with Raphael or Devon, if Raphael's not back yet, and he'll hear your testimony and decide in your best interests. Then you'll get your clothing back and the Destination Van will take you to your Final Destiny."

"This is unbelievable." Andrea shook her head. "What do I do in the meantime?"

"Your TV remote is in the pocket by your right arm. Or, if you prefer to read, we have an excellent library. There's also a music channel, and once you're on your feet, you'll be able to go down to the lounge and meet our other residents and visit the cafeteria." Joshua produced a folder. "In the meantime, here's a packet for you to read. This is only your first day, and I know it takes a while for everything to sink in, so I'll leave you for a bit. If you get hungry or have any questions, push the button on your left and I'll return." He handed it to her, then went out the door.

******

"How's our newest resident?" Jake, another Transitional Angel asked Joshua. "I hear she's quite a handful."

"They're always cranky when they wake up and realize they don't have wings and harps or lounging on a cloud. I've even had some who cry with relief, because they were expecting the fiery gates of Hell."

"That's what mine was expecting," Jake replied. "He actually woke up screaming, then realized he wasn't in the river Styx. Man cried for fifteen minutes and repented for everything he'd ever done. Hope he's still repentant when he meets with David next week."

"I know." Joshua nodded. "Mine's pretty angry and confused, but I think she'll come around. How long have we been doing this? I predict mine will be reaching her Final Destiny within the next month, unless of course, she discovers she likes it here better."

Jake shook his head. "Man, I hate that when it

happens. Remember Lex? Had to deprive him of everything until he got the message he had to choose."

"He was so mad at us." Both angels reflected on those with 'Transition-itis'.

"Anyway…" Joshua cleared his throat. "Donatello will have his hands full when Miss *Aundrea* demands she be sent to Heaven."

"Want to make a wager on who gets out of here the fastest?" Jake asked. "Winner gets first pick of clients."

"You know what will happen if Michael finds out…"

"He's got his hands full with tension in the Middle East," Jake added. "I have it on good authority he's not even reading the reports. As long as we don't act too pushy, and agree not to sabotage the other's efforts, like Bran and Zeke did several months ago."

"Agreed." Joshua shuddered as he recalled what had transpired. "I have no desire to work with the Mormans or dealing with their woes at not being given their own planet."

"Imagine Zeke dealing with the ones who think they will wake up surrounded by seven women!"

Both men grinned and shook hands. The bet was on.

Chapter Two

"But I don't see the need for this ridiculous discussion." Andrea pursed her lips. "Why is it so important to discuss my siblings? I'm the one who died."

"Because, as we found out yesterday, you felt your parents lavished all their love and attention on them. Did you bring that list I asked you to make?"

"No, I did not." Andrea raised her chin up. "I fail to see why a list of my sister and brother's good qualities vs bad is relevant to my being able to enter Heaven. For God's sake, my beloved Tony is waiting for me."

Donatello tapped his computer pad. "You're referring to Anthony Mueller? Ah yes…Mr. Mueller reached his Final Destination in the year two thousand thirteen in the year of Our Lord and chose to go to an Undisclosed Location."

"What the heck does that mean?" Andrea snapped. "Is that Heaven-speak for he's waiting for me?" She gripped the arms of the chair and leaned forward.

Donatello shook his head. "I'm sorry. It means he's gone somewhere private, and only Gabriel knows where he's gone."

"I insist to speak with this Gabriel, for where dear Tony goes, I go. He was the love of my life!"

"Ahem." Donatello coughed. "Now, back to your siblings, Paige and Sage."

"My parents had quite the sense of humor." Her tone was acidic. "Normal parents would have come up with 'Bill and Becky' or at least 'Amy and Andrew', but no.....they had to get cutesy. Do you know how many jokes about 'Page Turner' were told? Or if Sage was a weed, or if it meant he was highly intelligent?" She sniffed.

"You feel your siblings were teased? Or did it toughen them up?"

"Paige just laughed it off and thought it was because of her reading habits. Sage learned to use his fists on anyone who called him 'O Wise One'."

"How did you feel whenever Sage got into trouble?"

Andrea leaned back and smiled. "It showed me he wasn't going to let anyone walk all over him. Paige, on the other hand, would show her dimples and tilt her head, then watch everyone fall at her feet."

"Isn't that what life was like for you before she appeared?" Donatello asked.

Andrea pursed her lips. "I certainly didn't have to do that. All I had to do was ask for what I wanted. But suddenly, I had to compete with Paige."

"Compete. You were seven years older…in what ways were you rivals?"

"Suddenly everything I wanted, Paige had to have." Andrea scowled. "I had tickets to an NSync concert, but since Paige had decided Justin Timberlake was her man, guess who had to drag her ten-year-old sister along? It was embarrassing, especially since we had backstage passes. But Paige turned her big blue eyes and that rosebud pout onto the security guard, and he melted. Just let her inside, even without a ticket! Then, once inside she went all fangirl and pretended to faint when JT signed her t-shirt. While the rest of us were getting our CDs signed, little Paige was being taken to JT's suite, away from the noise." She paused. "Then bragged later at how JT had not only kissed her forehead, but had taken a selfie with her, and promised to send it. Did my picture appear with JT? No, just the rest of the band. The nerve of her, to monopolize him like that!"

"That would be upsetting, to be upstaged in that manner."

"All her life, Paige has managed to pull the wool over everyone's eyes, I tell you. Not mine; I see right through her." Andrea put her hands over her eyes and tried to calm down.

"Let's talk about Sage for a moment. Did you go to any of his athletic events?"

"Only one basketball game, but it was boring. Who wants to watch little boys running up and down a gym, shooting balls into baskets? Football is too cold, and baseball is too hot. Besides, I was busy with my own social life at the time."

"What about when he made the Olympic team?"

"I saw him off at the airport and cheered him on, of course. He did bring me a few nice souvenirs from the games."

"What about when your second husband, Jason Sterling, gave him an office in the company?"

"Darling Jason overestimated Sage's skills."

"Wasn't it Sage who discovered you were skimming money from the company?"

"That company had my name on it too, and I had every right to borrow a few hundred or so every month. I had an image to maintain." Andrea uncrossed her legs. "If Sage had kept his mouth shut, Jason wouldn't have divorced me."

"So, you harbor jealousy toward your sister and resentment toward your brother." Donatello tapped keys on his pad.

"I'm not jealous of Paige. I'm simply angry that she doesn't have to work hard to get what she wants. I—"

"—had to marry money," Donatello cut in. "Not once, but three times, with one narrowly escaping charges, and you feel Paige stole the limelight from you numerous times. Andrea, that's the definition of jealousy."

"Okay, okay. Maybe I was a little jealous," Andrea grumbled.

"Now we're making progress." Donatello closed his pad. "Ready for your next assignment?"

"Repeat the first one?"

"No. I want a complete list of all the men in your life. You can leave off your father and Sage, and any minor celebrities. I want a list of the men you loved, worked closely with, or worked for you. Can you have that ready for me by tomorrow?"

"What's that going to accomplish?" She narrowed her eyes at him. "You want to hear about my sex life? Are you that hard up, that you live vicariously through your clients?"

"Not at all. Doing so will show any patterns of behavior."

"Why is that important?" She bristled.

Donatello placed his pad on his desk and stood up. "All in due time. Now, time for your snack and to relax."

"But..." Andrea sputtered. "All I've done since being here is relax, rehash my life and relationships. What's next, how I treated the squirrels?" She rose to her feet when Donatello took her elbow. "I'm going. When can I talk to someone in charge about speeding this along?"

"We've been over this." Donatello's tone was mild, with a hint of irritation. "Raphael had an emergency in Brazil. We're not sure how long he'll be gone."

"Is it Fiesta season?" Andrea asked in a sarcastic manner. "Maybe he's partying."

"I highly doubt that. Homework, please, and I'll see you tomorrow." He ushered her from the room.

Another resident walking down the hall spotted her. "Hi Andi, I found out they're having a Mardi Gras night in the cafeteria. Beignets, Creole shrimp, gumbo, oysters, and mini-king cakes." The perky blonde linked her arm with Andrea's. "My mouth is just watering, thinking about it. Aren't you excited?"

Andrea attempted to dislodge her arm, to no avail. "Bitsy, I never cared for all that fattening food. I'm hoping to join my soulmate in Heaven, and I must look my best for him."

Bitsy's mouth dropped open. "Didn't they tell you? We're dead; we can't do anything about our weight. I can eat all the beignets I want, instead of counting sugars now. My diabetes is gone; there are no health problems here or wherever our Final Destination is."

Andrea blinked. "No weight gain? No irritating zits from eating too much chocolate?" The thought struck her. "What about my peanut allergy?"

"Eat as many as you like," Bitsy said. "No hives, no breathing issues. Didn't you read your handbook?"

"I skimmed it," Andrea lied, not wanting to admit she'd tossed it on a chair in her room and had promptly forgotten about it. "You would think Josh might have mentioned it."

"Oh, you have Josh? He's so dreamy." Bitsy clasped her hands and sighed. "Mine's Sam and he's a little grumpy." She shook her head. "I'm heading to the library for tea. Want to come?"

"Tea? In a library?"

"Yes. Today the Regency Room is spotlighting their books. Come on."

*****

"What you're telling me is, you slept with the man your sister was interested in, just because he didn't say hello to you?" Donatello pursed his lips as he looked up from his computer pad.

Andrea bristled. "Everyone said I looked beautiful at that party, but he barely even looked my way. I slipped a Xanax in his drink and followed him upstairs. To this day, he still thinks Paige only gave him a blowjob, because that's what she was doing when he woke up."

"Just what were you hoping to accomplish?"

Andrea lifted her chin. "I'm the oldest and wanted to make sure Paige was getting a man who knew what he was doing."

"Sounds more like revenge."

Andrea crossed her arms. "I was looking out for Paige, to make sure he was worthy of her affection."

"What about Number Fifteen on your list? You spent two weeks with him, then married your third husband a week later?"

"I needed to know if I was making the right choice," Andrea explained. "Jim had been coming on to me for weeks. How was I supposed to know he had a video camera in his room? He showed it to Trevor on our first anniversary, all because they decided to smoke weed and watch a movie from Jim's private collection. In his stoned state, Jim called up the wrong file, then tried to cover it up by saying it was someone who looked like me. Trevor confronted him after they'd sobered up and if Jim hadn't said my name, I think we would have gotten away with it."

"So far, you've been with men out of misplaced loyalty, revenge, boredom, dares, and general whim. Now, your homework for tonight is to bring me a list of everyone who's ever been hurt by your actions-the friends you've lost, relationships broken, all parties involved."

"I can't remember every party I've ever been to, Donatello." Andrea shook her head.

"People, Andrea. People you've hurt. Pay attention."

"Okay, okay." Pressing her lips together, Andrea looked peeved.

"I'll see you tomorrow." Donatello stood up, indicating the session was over.

Andrea, still smarting from his uncharacteristic outburst, escaped to her lounge, where she discovered reruns of *Dynasty*.

Chapter Three

Raphael laughed as Donatello vented his frustrations. "Sounds like quite a challenge."

Donatello bristled. "I take great pride in keeping calm, but that woman makes me want to strangle her, or at least, shake some sense into her. She's been spoiled all her life, manipulated everyone around her, and keeps demanding to be allowed into Heaven. We're almost finished with her self-analysis, but quite frankly," he paused for breath. "I don't think she's ready for the next step."

Raphael leaned back in his chair and steepled his fingers, absently stroking his dark mustache. "It's against policy, but if you'd like me to sit in on the next session…"

"Oh, yes." Breathing a sigh of relief, Donatello offered a quick prayer of thanks. "Maybe you'll see something I've missed. How was the Middle East crisis?"

Raphael smiled and leaned forward. "People are never going to change their beliefs until someone credible comes along, and unfortunately, the last one was several thousand years ago. If I were less honorable, I'd be tempted to write a parchment with a 'secret teaching' that could be authenticated and shake up the Islamic religion. Also the Hindus. It would avoid so many arguments when they wake up here."

"Definitely. Write one for the Mormans too."

Raphael nodded. "Anything else on your mind?"

"Not at the moment. Thanks for calming me down." Donatello leaned back against the couch and sighed. "None of my other clients are problems. Two are ready for their Final Destination tomorrow and my newest one is due to arrive this afternoon."

"Good, because I have a special assignment for you arriving next week. A young mother is about to miscarry, and you've done such a wonderful job with those precious cherubs. Aside from Ms Turner, I've lightened your caseload."

Donatello beamed. "It's both heartbreaking and refreshing to work with those young ones who don't understand what's going on. It will be a nice change of pace."

"I knew I could count on you." Raphael stood up. "I hear there's lasagna for dinner tonight, followed by karaoke in the Baroque Room."

Donatello frowned. "No karaoke for me. Last week, Gregory and his unit insisted on the most vile-I can't even call it music." He shuddered.

"That's why it's in the Baroque Room. Gregory won't set one foot in it. Come on, I think you deserve some fun."

*****

"Rafe!" Joshua waved at him to join his table. "Don, this concerns you too, so please join us."

Raphael grimaced. "Why do I have the feeling this concerns a certain diva?"

"Because it is. It always is. That woman is a menace, dead or alive." Joshua skewered his lasagna noodles as the others took a seat. He waited until the two men said a short prayer before eating and then he explained, "The food's not good enough. Why can't we have TV on demand, so she can watch *Dynasty* from the beginning, instead of Season Five. Why can't she have her jewelry? The list goes on and on. I tell you, it's a wonder no one killed her sooner."

Raphael held up his hand. "I'm sitting in on her next counseling session, in order to see for myself. Now, can we change the subject, so I'll have an open mind tomorrow?"

"One last thing…Did any of you peg her for a *Dynasty* fan? I thought she'd go for more of *Real Housewives* or something." Joshua laughed.

"Maybe Alexis Carrington was her role model or something," Raphael said.

"I pictured Joan Crawford," Donatello observed.

"She's not old enough." Raphael shook his head. "Jezebel?"

Joshua choked. "I doubt she's ever set foot in a church unless it was a major holiday or funeral."

Donatello took a drink of his soda. "Regardless, let me remind you we've had different people here before and they've all gone to their Final Destination in a timely manner. Can we please change the subject? Who wants to try the *Hallelujah Chorus* in about an hour?"

Joshua groaned. "I confess I want to try *Rock of Ages* that Bitsy insisted on blaring from her room last week."

The other two stared at him.

"What?" Joshua asked. "It's catchy. *Rise up, gather round*...I've been practicing."

"Any music produced by a deaf cheetah can't be any good." Donatello shuddered.

Raphael cleared his throat. "No one judges, Don. We're just going to blow off steam. New topic...Who wants to sign up for the new Baseball Protection League?"

*****

Andrea entered what she hoped would be her final day of Reflection. *Wonder what part of my sex life he wants to talk about this time?* With a smug smile, she settled herself in her customary chair, then her smile faded. Something was different, but what? Donatello's chair was empty, nothing looked out of place, but years of being the center of attention had given her an acute sense of awareness of being watched.

She glanced at the overhead light, the lamp on the desk, and the imposing statue of a winged angel, his wings outstretched. The angel faced her; had it always been there? Andrea couldn't remember. With a furtive look at the door, she rose from her seat and carefully repositioned the statue, so it faced the far corner. *That's better.* She returned to her seat and smoothed the wrinkles from her blue slacks. *Hopefully today, he'll finally agree to send me to Heaven!*

Donatello entered and greeted her. "Good news, Andrea. You only have two more sessions with me."

"Two?" She gasped. "I thought this would be our final one, since we've discussed everyone from my childhood to my business. What else is there?"

"You left out an important person. Francis Gillespi."

"Who?" Andrea blinked. "Oh, you mean Frank?"

"Yes, your manager. I'm curious as to why you never mentioned him."

"Oh my god," she scoffed. "He's not important. He's a manager, and I fire him at least once a week or more. Why do you need to know about him?"

Donatello raised an eyebrow. "You fire him every week, then rehire him? There has to be a reason he's been your employee for ten years."

Andrea pursed her lips. "He's an insufferable know-it-all who never knew when to keep his mouth shut, and thought his way was always the right one." Her tone icy, she continued. "However, he did a good job handling my financial affairs and household staff, so he wasn't entirely incompetent. But the man had to be put in his place when he overstepped his boundaries."

"Tell me why you don't feel he's a significant man in your life." Donatello tapped the keys on his pad.

Andrea blew out her breath. "I told you about the men I dated, slept with, and married—"

"Andrea," Donatello cut in. "You mentioned your butler, your chauffeur, the secretaries who worked under you at Mueller Enterprises, Sterling Publishing, Von Werner Shipping, and even the pool boy, all who only worked for you a short time. What I cannot fathom is you left out a person who has proved his loyalty for ten years."

"Because he refused to leave me alone," Andrea snapped. "He would always smile in that ingratiating way of his, then do the polar opposite of what I'd asked him to do." She leaned forward and gripped the arms of the wing-backed chair. "We had a deal; he would save the company and turn it around, then step down. Did he? No! Instead, he decided it was better to stay on as CFO, and put me on an allowance, if you can imagine the scandal. An allowance….as if I were twelve years old again."

"Yet, it had a lasting effect. The company thrived and stayed solvent, and you did become quite wealthy."

"That I did," she conceded. "But then I discovered the cancer."

"Why not fight it more? It says here you refused to do anything. I never pegged you for a quitter."

"I'm not a quitter! I saw the results of chemo, radiation, and what other treatments did, and I wanted—I wanted…" her voice broke.

"You cared more about looking good and playing on everyone's sympathy than your own health." Donatello's voice was gentle. "Still manipulating everyone to the end."

Andrea felt tears well up in her eyes. "Frank was the one person who saw through me, and he never gave up on me. Never. Even though I was horrible to him." She scrubbed away the few teardrops rolling down her cheek.

A soft tap came the door, then a stranger poked his head inside. "Is this a bad time, Donatello?"

"No, perfect timing as always, Rafe. I think Miss Turner has finally made a breakthrough." Donatello introduced his supervisor.

Mortified to be caught in tears, Andrea attempted to smile brightly at the newcomer. "Don't mind me. You know what it's like to re-evaluate everything. I'm just an emotional female."

Raphael took the other seat and gave her a nod. "No explanations necessary, Ms Turner. I make it a point to sit in on some of the final sessions, so if it's alright with you?"

"But of course." Andrea finished drying the moisture from her eyes and cheeks. "Donatello brought up the most fascinating detail… I'd left a member of my staff off his list. Can you imagine?" She giggled and put her fingers to her lips. "I don't know how I left out good ol' Frank."

Raphael glanced at Donatello and cleared his throat. "Sometimes we overlook those whom we didn't realize were the most influential."

"I wouldn't call him influential exactly."

"You were just explaining that he was the one person who never gave up on you," Donatello pointed out. "In your own words, neither your siblings, your parents, ex-husbands, ex-lovers, and even your employers offered any help when your cancer came to light. What I'm wondering now is, whom did you tell when you were diagnosed?"

"I didn't want to cause a fuss when there were bigger issues out there." Andrea smiled at Raphael. "I believe we announced it on the Von Werner Facebook page, and that was it."

"What would you consider 'bigger issues' other than your health?" Donatello asked. "Did the announcement also name a replacement for you?"

"Well, yes." Her smile faltered. She cleared her throat, clasped her fingers and continued, "My stepson Michael was named CEO and Frank would be working closely with him while I was indisposed. I'm surprised it's not in your file."

Donatello tapped more keys. "Yes, and there was a long thread of well-wishers, speculation as to why you were stepping down, since cancer was not mentioned. There is also documentation of some not-so-nice comments."

"No mention of my cancer?" Andrea's mouth dropped open in horror. "What exactly does it say?"

"Just that you were stepping down to deal with a health issue. Oh, here we go…about halfway down, someone mentioned the cancer."

"Who posted it?" Andrea demanded, feeling her control slip. "I left specific instructions. Damn it, Frank! I told you the man was an imbecile who wouldn't listen to me."

"Actually, this was posted by someone named Abby Normal." Donatello looked up. "Does that name sound familiar?"

"No." Andrea frowned. "I wonder if I could take a look at her profile?"

"I'm afraid that's against policy."

"How come you get to look at it? It's my life we're talking about here," Andrea challenged.

"Because it's our job," Raphael cut in. "Now I'm curious why you blamed Frank."

"Oh, I don't know." Andrea settled back and tried to calm down.

"You must have had some reason," Raphael replied. "First, you tell Donatello how worthless Frank is, but to me, he seems to be the most wonderful man in your life. Now you say he's incompetent. Which is it, Andrea?"

Andrea sat there, feeling her emotions churn. “I don’t understand why you need to know this.”

“Because it’s important.” His voice gentle, Raphael took the seat beside her. “Everyone who passes through Transition ends up facing some aspect of their lives which are unpleasant. In the end, it’s a huge relief to work through it and get rid of that weight.”

“What weight?” Andrea blew out a breath. “Just because I don’t think he’s worth discussing doesn’t mean he’s a burden.”

“There’s some reason you defend him one moment and lambast him the next,” Raphael pressed.

“Isn’t my hour about up?” she asked. “Surely, there is someone else who has a more interesting life to dissect.”

“No, you’re my final appointment of the day.” Donatello smiled. “What are you afraid of?”

“Nothing.” Her anger flared. “You want to know what happened? Fine. He took advantage of me during a weak moment, then refused to do anything more. Said he’d crossed a line, and it would never happen again. The nerve of him!”

Raphael and Donatello exchanged glances.

“What, no comment?” Andrea demanded. “I expected you to have some glib, new age insight or something.”

“I’m sorry Andrea. I’m just not seeing the problem. Let me get this straight.” Raphael steepled his hands in front of his lips. "You're saying Frank caught you being vulnerable– and I take it you mean intimately–then refused your attempts to further the relationship?" He looked at Donatello and held out his hand.

The other angel silently handed over the computer pad.

Andrea felt tears welling up again amid her fury. "No matter what I offered him-money, position, status-he refused to be anything other than my employee. Can you imagine?"

Raphael's mouth twitched. "I'd say you finally met a man you couldn't manipulate, buy, or control, and that's the crux of your anger." He handed the tablet back to Donatello and tapped his chin. "Here's what I propose for tomorrow's session. Let's meet in Handel's Hall at the usual time and take it from there."

"Handel's Hall? Where's that?" Andrea relaxed a bit. With the change of rooms, maybe this was a good sign?

Raphael stood up. "Joshua will fill you in after breakfast. It was most enlightening to meet you, Ms Von Werner." After shaking her hand, he opened the door and departed.

Donatello also stood, indicating the session was over. "Enjoy your evening, Andrea, and I'll see you tomorrow."

Excitement filled her veins. Maybe she was about to finally be reunited with Tony?

Chapter Four

Handel's Hall turned out to be a large room filled with gilt furniture and decorated with musical notes, instruments, and music lyrics on the wall. Andrea spotted a line from her favorite Elton John song above a gold and white upright piano.

A gigantic mirror occupied one end of the room. Rafe stood up from one of the many chairs clustered in front of it and motioned to her.

Smoothing the wrinkles of her tunic, Andrea approached with caution. This would be the first time seeing herself before death, and she wasn't sure she was ready.

"What kind of mirror is that? I don't see anything reflected." Not knowing whether to be relieved or disappointed, Andrea seated herself beside Donatello.

"This is called the Mirror of Opportunity. We're going to show you snippets of your life before you make your decision. Are you ready?"

"Decision? I already know." Andrea jabbed her thumb at Donatello. "I've been telling him for a week now that I want to go to Heaven to be with my beloved Tony."

"That's all well and good, but we still have to follow procedure."

Tapping her foot, Andrea closed her eyes and fumed before cooperating. The mirror wavered, then showed a picture of a little girl wearing a pink dress, matching socks, and white Mary Jane shoes, with a yellow cardboard crown on her head.

"My fifth birthday! All my friends came to my party, and we took turns riding a pony." Andrea smiled at the memory, having recalled the story often.

Her smile faded when she saw herself taking turn after turn on the pony, then sticking out her tongue and pouting until it was her turn again.

"What… wait…wait a minute… what am I doing? That was never a part of the story." Andrea watched in dismay as her five-year-old self tossed a rock at the pony, then ducked behind a tree. The pony reared, nearly throwing off a little boy who had just mounted. Children screamed, and Andrea reappeared on the other side of the 'camera', dress hitched halfway up her back as she tugged her slip out of her underwear.

"You weren't caught, because you claimed to have been in the bathroom," Raphael explained. "Your slip being caught in your panties was very convincing."

Stunned, Andrea watched as the handler calmed the pony, then lifted the little boy into the saddle again. "I don't remember that at all." She watched herself being led away by her mother to put her dress back in place.

The mirror wavered, and this time showed Andrea on the playground, alone on the swing set while the other children ran around.

"Recall any of this?" Donatello asked.

Andrea frowned. "Every time I tried to join in, the other kids would stop and go somewhere else." Unexpected pain lanced her heart. "I never knew why."

"One little girl had seen you throw the rock. She told the others, and since children see everything 'right' or 'wrong', they didn't want to be around you."

"But… I had plenty of friends in school," Andrea protested. "The twins were born when I was seven, and all my friends came to their second birthday party."

"Children also have a remarkable ability to forgive and forget. Something that changes as we grow older." Rafe cleared his throat. "Let's fast-forward a bit." The mirror wavered again.

"Oh no, not that infamous concert." Andrea closed her eyes and leaned back. "I already know how this plays out."

"Do you? Please watch."

Opening one eye, then the other, Andrea watched herself shove Paige into the back seat of the sedan and saw the girl crying, with her hands over her ears the entire drive.

"Why is she doing that?"

"You had the volume up so loud, it hurt her ears. Paige continued to suffer from tinnitus well into her adult years, needing hearing aids at age thirty."

"I just thought she wasn't paying attention. I ruined Paige's hearing?"

"Unfortunately, yes. When you went backstage, Paige was relieved to finally be in a quiet room, and convinced Justin to give her some Tylenol and a wad of cotton for each ear."

"She never said a word. I mean, we all had trouble hearing after the concert. That's normal." Andrea chewed her lip and looked down. "Poor Paige. I had no idea."

Donatello cleared his throat. "If we can continue?"

Andrea watched in shock as she observed herself stealing her so-called friends' boyfriends when she herself was dateless or feeling down. But when the mirror showed her friends' point-of-view, her mood shifted from righteous indignation to shame, an emotion becoming more familiar each day.

After viewing her carefree fling with the male stripper at her bachelorette party, she burst into tears.

"Stop, please.... I don't want to see any more." Sobbing, Andrea buried her face in her arms as she turned away from the treacherous mirror. "I'm never getting into Heaven, am I?" She sniffed.

A gentle hand rubbed her shoulder.

"You've made a major breakthrough, Andrea, by admitting you made mistakes." Raphael's soothing voice broke through her pity-party. "It's never too late to make atonements."

"H-how?" She sat up and blew her nose with the tissues Donatello provided. "I'm dead…." A fresh wave of grief hit her.

"That's something we'll discuss when we're finished here." Raphael handed her more tissues.

"There's more?" Andrea turned her watery eyes to face Raphael's concerned face. "Can't you just take my word for it? I've been a horrible person who doesn't deserve to be with my beloved." She blew her nose again.

"Unfortunately, no. We need to keep going. But you've admitted mistakes, so the next part should be quick."

The mirror shimmered and Andrea cringed when she observed her drunken self sleeping with the pool boy six months into her marriage, and her own justification when adjusting the checkbook to cover her spending spree.

"Stop for a moment," Andrea demanded angrily. "I needed new clothes for the Grand Opening, and I put that money back."

"Yes, but the next time…" Donatello activated the mirror and showed a split screen of Andrea doing the same thing ten more times. "Each time you told yourself you'd replace the funds, but as time went on, it became easier to take it out, rather than to put it back in. Eventually, you stopped caring, and blamed it on other people's mistakes. Watch."

Anxiety medication became part of her morning routine, as was habitually double-checking all the books.

"You nearly developed an ulcer, trying to remember all the lies you were telling."

"I don't remember that. Is it possible this thing is wrong?" Andrea continued to watch. "Oh, that's when Tony had his heart attack. Where am I? I know I rushed to his bedside."

The mirror shimmered and showed her lying face down, covered with a sheet and ignoring her phone.

"That spa cost me over a thousand dollars," Andrea protested. "I couldn't just walk out."

"Yet, you still had a private session after hours in the pool."

"He was consoling me." Andrea watched as she observed herself and the aesthetician frolicking in the heated pool. A shiver went through her as she remembered her first time in the water.

"Andrea." Raphael's mild tone brought her back to the present. "Shall we continue?"

"I—yes." Andrea shook her head and watched the mirror shimmer. Tears formed as she watched the awful argument which led to the public divorce. Following that, her own slide into depression, which resulted in getting her therapist fired for spending the night with her. Her whirlwind romance and marriage to Jason Sterling, only to divorce him six months later.

"Let's pause here a moment." Raphael sat

back and tapped his chin. "Why did you divorce Jason?"

"He slept with the maid." Andrea lifted her chin. "In our bed. Plus, I caught her wearing the emeralds Jason bought me, or so I thought. Turned out he'd bought us both the same necklace. I fired her and kicked him out of the house."

"You're sorry you stole from and cheated on your first husband, but you were outraged when the tables were turned?" Raphael asked her. "Doesn't that seem a little hypocritical?"

"You're a man. Of course, you wouldn't understand."

"Here's what I see. I see a young woman who learned to manipulate everyone around her, and when she didn't get her way, she lashed out at the most opportune victim. 'Hurt them before they hurt me' became your motto, subconsciously speaking, since you felt betrayed by your parents when your siblings were born. You couldn't bear to share their love and attention, so you focused on doing everything your way."

Stunned, Andrea could only gape at him.

"Did I cut too close? That's what your therapist told you, isn't it? You tried to prove him wrong, but the only thing you succeeded in doing was to get him fired."

"Bert was weak." Andrea defended, jolted from the shock. "He thought he was so smart, but underneath all that bravado was the heart of a coward. Spineless idiot."

"Okay." Donatello stepped forward. "Let's take a break for lunch."

Andrea bolted from her chair and fled the room, not stopping until she reached a quiet corner. Emotions assaulted her. Anger, remorse, confusion, guilt, and anxiety ran the gamut. Who knew dying would lead to this?

Andrea had always pictured dying, then being reunited with her Soul Mate and living happily ever after in the warm love of whatever Supreme Being happened to be in charge. *But now, it looks as if I'm not going there.* Terror hit her stomach. If she wasn't going to Heaven—*oh, no!* She had no desire to be a tortured soul in the tenth circle of Hell or doomed to be on the River Styx. "No, no, I'm not-NO!"

Running to her room, Andrea pushed past the others and slammed the door. Falling on her bed, she hugged her pillow and rocked back and forth.

There had to be a way out. Snatching up her Welcome Packet, Andrea skimmed until she found the staff listing. Gabriel's name was first; that meant he was in charge. Gabriel. She needed to talk to Gabriel. Calmer, she took several cleansing breaths before releasing her hold on her pillow and tore open one of the cleansing towelettes to erase the puffiness from her eyes.

Taking a firm grip on her courage, she ventured to the cafeteria. She looked around for Bitsy but didn't see her. After getting her food, she took a spot at the first available table.

"Did you hear the news about Bitsy? She Transitioned this morning." A woman sat down beside her.

"Really? Anyone know where she went?" Andrea cut into her juicy steak.

"Oh, we never ask that, dear. It's not polite. We'll just feast tonight at her Transition Party and be happy for her."

"There's a party? I wasn't invited."

The woman looked shocked. "You don't have to be invited. Didn't you read your handbook?"

"I've been very busy with my Transitional counselor; I can't remember everything." Andrea took another bite of her succulent meat. "Where is it being held and at what time?"

"Regency Library. It was her favorite place, so we're honoring her with High Tea and plenty of chocolate. She was a romance author, you know. New York Times Best Seller several years in a row." The other woman beamed.

Andrea made a face. "I was more of a Jackie Collins fan."

"We'll see tonight after Vespers. Oh, there's Sheila." The woman stood up and picked up her tray to move to the other table.

Vespers? Oh right, the evening prayer service. After the trauma of the past two days, Andrea seriously considered attending. "Yes, of course. See you tonight."

As she ate her lunch, Andrea reflected on what

she'd seen and speculated what else she was going to see.

Remorse filled her as she ate in solitude. Was everything she remembered about her childhood wrong? Sure, she'd made some questionable choices in her teens and young adulthood, but surely the statute of limitations had expired on those? Everyone made mistakes when they were young…surely it wouldn't keep her from being reunited with Tony!

A bell chimed, and she recognized it as the gentle reminder lunch was over. Gathering her tray, she placed it on the appropriate conveyor belt and returned to Handel's Hall.

While she waited for Raphael and Donatello to appear, she wandered around admiring the furniture, pictures, and reading the snippets of song lyrics.

"Ready, Andrea?"

She looked up at the sound of Donatello's voice. "I-yes. I was admiring all the musicians whose lyrics are quoted."

Raphael smiled. "The reason you're seeing song lyrics means music plays a firm part of your memories."

Andrea blinked. "You mean…?"

"Yes. Most people only see the music scores. There are no words anywhere in here."

A shiver went through her. "That's so freaky." She rubbed her arms.

Raphael and Donatello waited until she made her way closer.

"Not really." Donatello explained. "Freaky was

when we had a woman who claimed she hear Mozart playing the piano. She swore she could hear *Ein A Klein A Nacht Muzik* the entire time."

Andrea took her seat and shuddered. "Before we get started again, I was wondering if I could speak to Gabriel. I believe he's in charge around here?"

Donatello and Raphael exchanged glances.

"Gabriel is still unavailable at the moment," Raphael said. "May I ask why you want an audience with him? You're nearly finished with your evaluation of your life and ready for the next step."

"I see how this is going." Andrea tried to control her anxiety. "I've been a horrible person at times, and I don't deserve to go to Heaven. But if I plead my case to Gabriel and make him see that I'm eternally sorry for what I've done…I do remember hearing about God's mercy, about murderers being Born Again and getting into Heaven, wouldn't that apply to me?" She blinked back tears as her voice squeaked on the final word.

Raphael shrugged his shoulders. "As I said, he is on assignment, covering an emergency on Earth. You are correct though. God's mercy extends to everyone who is truly repentant. I understand your fear and can assure you this process does not mean you are being sent to the Dark One. Most of the souls enjoy reliving their memories, especially ones they've forgotten."

She slowly let out her breath. "I'm not going to Hell?"

"That's usually not our standard practice. You woke up here, which means Our Lord saw something redeeming in you. Otherwise, the Dark One would have claimed you. But you must complete the process before moving on. Do you think you can, or would you prefer to finish this tomorrow?"

Andrea sighed. "No, let's keep going. The sooner we finish, the sooner I'll get to see Tony." She turned her attention to the mirror again. "Oh, my god-goodness.... Thad Von Werner." Andrea corrected herself and put her hand to her lips. "My father-in-law. What's he doing?"

"Showing your third husband Trevor the prenuptial agreement, he wants you to sign."

Andrea got angry. "I never signed anything, though that old goat tried to claim I had."

"Actually," Donatello cut in. "You did sign it. You just didn't know it." He nodded at the screen.

Andrea watched in horror as she signed a stack of papers without reading them. "I remember that day." Shock constricted her throat. "Trevor came to see me with a stack of stock reports I needed to sign. I always had to sign them every month.... He slipped it in with them and I never noticed?" She clapped her hand over her mouth.

"Trevor kept it in his safe, which had been destroyed in the house fire. Otherwise, he would have been disowned by his family, and he didn't think you would have married him otherwise."

"Probably not," Andrea admitted. "I had no intention of creating another Jason situation. But if

Trevor had been smarter, he would have given his father a copy, or kept it in the safe deposit box."

"Yet, with no proof after Trevor's death, your court battle was over as soon as Frank entered your life."

Andrea winced. "Don't remind me. Oh wait, you're going to anyway."

The mirror shimmered and Andrea gritted her teeth as she watched herself interview, flirt with, hire, fire, and argue with Frank Gillespi multiple times. "I could not figure that man out," she fumed. "Oh no, this is when he made me go to the doctor." She watched as she slowly lost weight, underwent treatment, and ultimately leaned on Frank for support. "Do you have to show this part?"

"It's all part of your life. Frank brought out your long-buried gentle side, the side where you finally acknowledged you needed someone and allowed them to help you, without demanding anything in return."

Andrea watched the mirror fade to dark. "What now? My funeral?"

"If you want to see it, yes. We'll be happy to show it tomorrow when we move to the next phase."

"Why not now?" Puzzled, Andrea looked at the two angels in turn.

"You've had an emotional day, and it's time for some self-care." Donatello rose to his feet and took her by the hand. "You now have an appointment in the Celestial Spa, for a soothing massage and whatever else you need."

Andrea felt her spirits perk up. "Celestial Spa? Why was I not told of it when I first arrived?"

Raphael closed the doors behind them. "We found out in the past two hundred years that women-and some men-would spend every day in it, rather than do their homework. Now we reserve the spa for the more emotional days. Just as the library and recreational rooms are restricted for the same reason. Don will show you the way to the spa and we'll see you tomorrow after breakfast."

*****

"Are we really going to show her that footage?" Donatello asked. "You saw her reaction to Frank…. what do you think will happen when she sees the footage of the eulogy?"

"She's going to be furious, but it will fuel her desire for the next step."

"Andi still thinks she's going to Heaven." Donatello looked uncertain. "What happens if she refuses?"

"Then we tell her the truth."

Chapter Five

Andrea awakened the next morning, full of curiosity and excitement. After viewing what she hoped was the largest funeral in the town's history, she would finally be reunited with her beloved Tony and live happily ever after, reclining on a cloud in Heaven.

She took her time during breakfast, savoring everything and hoping the food in Heaven was as scrumptious. By now, she was one of the residents who had been in Transition the longest and answered the questions of the newcomers.

Joshua sought her out, to let her know of a slight change in her daily routine. An appointment was available if she wanted to visit the spa before going to Handel's Hall, but she needed to let him know.

"Of course. Can I still go afterward?"

"Yes. I'll make all the arrangements." Joshua hurried out the door.

After gossiping with a new arrival over coffee, Andrea seethed with anger as she headed toward the spa. "Imagine! My mansion's been sold, and the company bought out?" She accepted a cup of chamomile tea and placed her feet in the warm water.

"How do you know that?" Natasha, another resident, asked her.

"I met a newcomer who recognized me from the internet and told me about hearing it on the morning news, about an hour before she crashed her car." Andrea set her cup down with a bang. "I wonder if Donatello knows? Frank and my stupid brother are behind this, I know."

"Why do you say that?" Natasha asked.

"Andrea," her esthetician interjected. "Now is not the time for such talk. You need to calm down, not worry about what's going on down there. It's out of your control."

With a huff, Andrea settled back in her chair and nodded at Natasha, then plastered what she hoped was a serene look on her face.

After admiring her pretty pink toenails, Andrea said goodbye to Natasha and made her way down to Handel's Hall.

The doors were locked, to her surprise. "What's going on?" Andrea tugged at the doors, then knocked. "I don't remember if there's another door." She walked down the width of the building but couldn't find another entrance.

Frustrated, Andrea returned to the doors and tried again, to no avail.

"Andrea."

Whirling around, she felt relieved to see Raphael walking toward her.

"There's been another unexpected delay," he said.

"What now?" Agitated, she banged her fists on the door. "What could possibly be more important than me seeing my own funeral, then moving on?" Her voice rose with every word.

"Andrea, lower your voice." Raphael tried to take her arm.

She yanked free. "No, you listen to me. I've been patient with all the rehashing of my life, and seeing things I hadn't known, but I learned today everything I've worked so hard for is gone. Gone. G-O-N-E! I want to know if they auctioned it off over my cold, dead body, and if Frank and Sage are out there celebrating my demise." Tears streamed down her face as her voice squeaked. "I've been here the longest. I want to be reunited with Tony. Take me to Gabriel." She sank to the floor and covered her face. "Just take me to Gabriel."

Raphael knelt beside her and put his arm around her as she sobbed. When the storm was over, he produced tissues for her eyes. "Now, will you come with me? I think we owe you an explanation, and in fact, you may be able to help us."

"H-help you? You? How?" Andrea felt a surge of hope in addition to the confusion.

Raphael helped her to her feet and escorted her down to Donatello's office. "Have a seat. We're about to do something unprecedented here in Transition. We can't show your funeral to you, because, as of this moment, you are alive on Earth." He seated himself at the desk.

Andrea blinked. "Excuse me? I'm alive?"

"Yes. The timeline, as of last night, was altered somehow, and you are very much alive."

Donatello cleared his throat. "It seems Tony has now been stricken with cancer and is about to die.... but we can't have the two of you here at the same time, for obvious reasons."

"How—how did this happen?" Andrea whispered.

"We don't know. We've sent for Gabriel and Michael to help sort this out. I've even sent Andrew, another one of our angels, down there, to help prolong the process, so he doesn't die before we get things fixed."

"I still don't understand. How can I be alive down there?" Andrea clutched her hands together.

The intercom crackled. Raphael jumped up and went to the door. An elderly man entered, his white hair flowing to his shoulders, contrasting with his closely cropped beard. He greeted Andrea and apologized for being away, "I've been trying to help with some of the tensions in the Middle East, when your situation came to my attention." Gabriel seated himself beside her. "Here is what we know. Anthony Mueller was able to return to his timeline just prior to your marriage and managed to disrupt your timeline. I'm amazed you even exist here at all; we're in uncharted territory. Long story short, while at your funeral, people began disappearing, as the timeline was disrupted. I managed to freeze your timeline but wasn't able to freeze the alternative one."

"How is this even possible?" Andrea exclaimed. "Can't anyone do anything?"

"Normally, timelines don't crisscross this way," Raphael explained. "Each choice made creates a new timeline, and normally if someone does alter their destiny, it simply causes a sense of déjà vu, or causes reports of doppelgangers to appear. Humans have a saying that everyone has a twin. There's some truth to it; the future is fluid, so if a person alters the timeline, the 'old' person feels compelled to move away, with no memory of their prior life. I know this sounds confusing, or like a bad science fiction show, but I'm trying to explain it in a way that makes sense."

"What happens now?" Donatello asked.

Gabriel laced his hands together. "We're going to do the same thing." He turned to Andrea. "I understand you've completed your review of your life, and have done some things you regret?"

"Y-yes." Andrea gulped, still trying to wrap her head around what was being said.

"Then I want to give you the opportunity to change things. I can only assume Tony returned with full knowledge, so you will too. Unfortunately, you don't get to pick your moment; we need to send you back to the exact same moment Tony was, in hopes that everything will return to normal. I have no idea which one of you will arrive here first, but since both of you have already been here, a note will be placed on your file, and you'll advance immediately to your Final Destination. Understand?"

Andrea could hardly comprehend it. "I think so."

"Good. You cannot mention this, however. People will turn you into a media circus and want to know all about your near-death experience. If you do mention it— "

"Don't worry," she cut him off. "I had enough media coverage during the divorce. If I get to go back and not make the same mistakes, I'll gladly keep my mouth shut about this place," Andrea promised.

"Okay. Here's what we're going to do. Enjoy your final night in Transition, then when you wake up tomorrow, you'll be twenty-four again, and about to marry Tony. You'll have all your memories of what took place before, and what you want to change. Periodically, you'll see me as I check up on you, so don't be alarmed. It's just a precaution, to make sure the timeline is being carried out. Enjoy this second chance, Andrea. Not many people get this opportunity."

Andrea let out the breath she hadn't realized she was holding. "I will. Thank you."

"Don't thank me yet," he cautioned. "Your future may still have a different ending. That's why it's so unpredictable. Just go live your best life." Gabriel helped her to her feet and ushered her out the door.

"Can I still get my massage and farewell party tonight?"

Gabriel looked at the other two angels, then back at Andrea. "Yes, but no mention of where you're really going."

"Don't worry. I've talked about Tony so much; everyone knows I'm going to be reunited with him." Head held high, Andrea sauntered off toward the spa.

*****

"What a crazy turn of events." Donatello sighed. "Gabriel, are you positive this will work?"

"The only thing is, we'll have to review her every move at the end of each day or week, to make sure she stays the course." Gabriel sank into the chair Andrea had vacated. "Michael is looking into who let Tony return, and where he went wrong. Hopefully, Andrea will make smarter choices and the two timelines will merge into one."

"And if they don't?"

"I don't even want to consider a third option right now. What say you we raid the staff cafeteria? I'm dying for a rare steak with all the trimmings."

"Too much lamb in the Middle East, eh?" Raphael clapped him on the back as he passed. "Time travel makes me hungry too."

"I didn't even know it was possible!" Gabriel exclaimed.

Chapter Six

June, 2006

Andrea opened her eyes to unfamiliar surroundings. Instead of the sterile look of her Transition room, the walls were a soft heather gray, with sunlight streaming in both corner windows.

I'm back! I'm really back! Andrea stretched out her toes, delighting in the silky feel of three-hundred-count Egyptian cotton again. *Ahhhhh….*

"Andrea!" The door burst open, and Paige bounded in to pounce on her bed. "Can you believe this day is finally here?"

"What are— "Andrea caught herself and beamed at her younger sister. "Looking forward to getting my room?"

Paige sucked in her breath. "You-you wouldn't mind? I'm tired of sharing a bathroom with Sage. Last week, you were furious when Mummy suggested it."

Andrea reached for her sister's hand. "Don't be silly. Tony and I are going to live happily ever after, and the only time we'll be here is when we're visiting. Why not let you have this room? Mama can turn yours into a guest room."

"That's what she said." Paige squeezed her hand. "Are you excited?"

"Very." Andrea lay back and sighed. So happy indeed. Now to correct all the mistakes she'd made the first time.

Several hours later, at the church, she and her seven bridesmaids posed for playful photos while dressing, then the more formal ones. Twenty minutes before the ceremony was to begin, Andrea steeled herself when a knock summoned her to the door.

"Hey baby." Tony's best man smiled down at her. "One more for old time's sake?"

Andrea fluttered her lashes as she remembered the excitement of groping each other in the broom closet. "Now Cole, it just wouldn't be right with me in my wedding finery."

"Yes but think of the excitement of me standing up there beside Tony, knowing I've had you one last time." His left hand slid over her right hip and stroked her backside.

"Cole, no. I've decided to turn over a new leaf." Reaching back, she removed his hand.

He snorted. "You? Right. We'll see how long this lasts." He pivoted and walked away.

Andrea retreated inside the changing room and tried to calm the flutters in her stomach.

"Getting nervous, sweetie?" Her mother stepped through the door.

"A little," Andrea lied.

"It will go by fast, and before you know it, you

and Tony will be off to Zurich for fun and relaxation after these past hectic months."

A knock sounded, and her father poked his head in. "Showtime, ladies. Muriel, they're ready to seat you."

Mrs. Turner squeezed her daughter's hand and left, already dabbing at her eyes. Paige gave her a quick kiss as did the rest of the bridesmaids before hurrying out of the room.

Andrea adjusted her veil and smoothed her voluminous ball gown skirt. Taking deep breaths, she tried to calm herself.

Soon, her father returned, his eyes glistening. "You look beautiful." He cleared his throat. "Ready?"

"Yes, Daddy."

*****

An hour later, she gazed into Tony's eyes as they swayed to the music of Kelly Clarkson.

"I love you so much, Tony. I'm so happy we did this."

"I'm simply happy you showed up after that horrendous fight we had last night at the rehearsal. Was Claudia upset when you switched her with Paige this morning?"

"I really don't know what I was thinking, making Paige walk down the aisle with Sage. She's had a crush on Greg ever since she met him several months ago."

"They seem to be getting along." The song ended and the tinkling of glassware began. Tony dipped her and planted a solid kiss on her lips before letting her back up.

"When do we leave for the honeymoon?" Andrea squeezed his hand as they headed back to the table.

"Tonight, we stay here, then tomorrow, we leave for that Caribbean resort you've talked about for the past nine months." Tony grinned at her.

Andrea gasped, then squealed.

Tony kept smiling. "I know I said that mountain cabin in Zurich, but I changed my mind."

"Thank you so much," she whispered and hugged him again before taking her seat.

*****

Two years passed. Andrea stayed true to her word and steered clear of temptation, even when the Grand Opening arrived. Tony shocked her by thrusting a brand-new credit card in her hand and telling her to buy herself something new.

Something's changed; Tony's not wrapped up in his work, and he's acting more loving toward me.

Still, Andrea went with a more conservative outfit and didn't get too extravagant.

Another year passed, and Andrea watched Tony's health like a hawk. The month of his heart attack loomed, and he began eating healthier and spent more time in the health club. Tony seemed happy, healthy, and appeared to actually enjoy her company as they rode the stationary bike and hiked on matching treadmills. Tony had programmed the Grand Canyon on his, while Andrea strolled the streets of Venice or walks on the beach.

As she finalized the details of Tony's fortieth birthday party, her housekeeper announced an unexpected guest.

"He wishes to speak to you privately, ma'am."

"Have him wait in the library and I'll be right there." Andrea finished the list she and her secretary were working on, then excused herself.

She was shocked when she saw him. "I'm so sorry to keep you waiting-Donatello! What a surprise. Please, have a seat." Andrea seated herself on the couch and watched as he took the leather chair. "Can I offer you any refreshments?"

"No thank you. I have to say, I'm rather impressed by the way the past three years have gone, Andrea. I feel as if I'm seeing a whole new you."

Andrea smiled. "Spending time with you and reflecting on my life…my past life showed me how selfish I've been, and I don't want to lose Tony. I'm determined to do things differently, and you know what? It's a brand-new life we've created." She told Don about the new lifestyle, and how happier things had been between them. "Did you ever find out who started this whole mess?"

Donatello nodded. "We're fairly certain

another Transitional Angel was involved. Gabriel is still sorting things out, but we will get to the bottom of it soon." He gestured with his hands. "No regrets, Andrea?"

"Absolutely none. The next hurdle is to not contract cancer in ten more years. If Tony and I can die peacefully in our sleep, and end up with you at the same time…" The thought struck her. "I know you said we'd go straight to Heaven, but is it possible to see our funerals?"

"I don't know." Donatello held up his hands. "We're in uncharted territory, so to speak."

Andrea bit her lip. "I'd like to go straight to Handel's Hall, though the spa was also nice. And the cafeteria."

"I get the picture." Donatello stood up. "I'll probably check in with you again in a few years. Keep up the good work."

Andrea rose from her seat and accompanied him to the door. "I will. Thank you so much."

*****

"Amazing what seeing your life through another's eyes can do," observed Donatello. "I honestly thought Andrea would only last a month at best before reverting to her old self."

"Gabriel figured it would only take three months." Raphael looked up from the monitor. "Now the betting pool is who dies first."

Donatello clicked his tongue. "How's Elijah doing in Transportation?"

Raphael grimaced. "The only thing I've heard was he wasn't very happy about being demoted, but like Gabriel said, he shouldn't have played with time like that. Now both timelines are finally merging, Eli seems hopeful he'll be allowed back in his old office."

"That's strictly up to Gabriel and Michael. According to what I've heard, Eli may never get his old position back, unless something drastic happens."

"Which is a shame. Eli was well-liked on Karaoke night. Dude can't sing to save his life but get enough Jaeger in him and he belts out a hilarious rendition of *Lose Yourself.*"

"Gah." Raphael gasped. "He raps?"

"Badly, but the crowd eats it up."

Epilogue

"We are gathered here today to celebrate the lives of Andrea and Anthony Mueller, who were wonderful active members of our community. Tony's company made many philanthropic contributions to our town, and Andrea was a generous, gracious hostess...." The pastor's voice went on to praise both of them.

Paige stood up and read letters to her sister from her children and other comments left on the funeral home's social media site. Songs were sung, and one of Tony's friends spoke about his friendship with the couple.

Up in Handel's Hall, Andrea and Tony clasped hands as they watched.

Occasionally, a tear rolled down Andrea's cheek. "I had no idea Paige could sing like that. Too bad, I couldn't have gone back sooner—oops!" She clapped her hand over her mouth and looked at Donatello, who winced.

"Wait-you went back too?"

The shock in Tony's voice caused her to snap her head back to face him. "What do you mean, 'too'?" Andrea gaped at him. "I went back to save our marriage."

"What are you talking about? I went back to save our marriage and to keep you from getting skin cancer."

"How did you know about that?" Realization washed over her. "You're the one who altered the timeline."

"You know about that?" Tony looked stunned.

Andrea snatched her hand away. "I was all set to demand I join you in the afterlife when Raphael told me about people disappearing at my funeral. That's why they sent me back to the night before we got married."

"I went back to right before my health began to get bad, in order to take better care of myself so I wouldn't die on you. I saw what happened to you after I died."

"Oh my god. They showed you that?" Andrea shrieked.

"Not all of it." Tony took her hand and explained, "I just wanted to check up on you, so I convinced my Transition Counselor, Eli, not to send me anywhere just yet, and we'd check in on you periodically. But when you refused to go through chemo, I knew I had to save you somehow."

"How did Eli manage to disrupt the timeline?" Raphael frowned.

Tony looked confused. "Eli said it wouldn't disrupt it. What do you mean?"

"You suddenly arrived here just as Andrea had

reached this stage," Donatello explained. "We'd never dealt with this type of issue before, and not knowing how the timeline was affected, we picked a random beginning point that was important to Andrea."

"I-I don't know anything about that," Tony spluttered. "Did Eli get in trouble?"

"He's been punished, and I hope we never have to deal with this issue ever again." Raphael crossed his arms over his chest. "Transition is a place to reflect, defend, and move on, not reflect and make changes. For you two, we're going to skip the Afterlife Survey and just send you on your way." He produced a packet of papers and handed one sheet to each. "Andrea, since the spa is your favorite place, you have one last appointment tonight. Tony, your tee-off time at the golf course begins in ten minutes. Tomorrow, I'll see you both by the fountain in the courtyard."

"There's a fountain? I never knew that." Andrea rose from her seat.

Tony took her elbow and escorted her from the room.

*****

"I'm glad we'll finally be together." Andrea leaned her head against Tony's shoulder. "Being here the first time without you was miserable."

"I know what you mean." Tony's arm tightened around her waist. "Watching you make mistake after mistake wasn't fun either. I knew I had to save you from yourself."

"I wonder what happened to Frank?" Andrea chewed her lip. "I meant to ask Donatello but forgot."

The shuttle they were in slowed, and another passenger climbed aboard.

Tony chuckled. "Frank was a Guardian Eli sent to watch over you. You never noticed he disappeared every Sunday? He had to recharge every seven days in order to stay corporeal."

Her eyes rounded at hearing this news. "Now that you mention it, he was hard to find at times." Andrea then sighed. "I was so horrible to him."

"He got you through your illness. Oh look, they actually do have pearly gates." Andrea's mouth dropped open in awe at the exquisite gates, gleaming white with thousands of pearls draped across the arches, creating a lacy effect. "It's beautiful!"

The shuttle stopped again, and the driver checked his manifest. "Everyone off, folks. Welcome to Heaven."

Part Two:

Saving Paige

Prologue

Francis Gillespi looked at his agenda and smiled. She'd done it. Andrea had curbed her selfish tendencies and managed to rewrite her future. She and Tony were off to their Final Destination, and his action in her previous life now a distant memory.

He looked at his next assignment and groaned. Getting up, he walked down the short hallway to his supervisor Leonardo's office.

"As if I've not been punished enough… now Paige?"

Leonardo swiveled around in his chair. "She was a wreck after Andrea's death, and since you already knew the family history, we thought you would be the best choice. You don't agree?"

Francis sank down into a chair and ran a hand through his hair. "Admittedly, Paige isn't as difficult as her sister. But an intervention is still an intervention. It says here she's drinking, gambling, and 'engaging in unhealthy behavior'… what the heck does that mean?"

"It means she's going down a path of self-destruction, and we need you to stop it, and get her back on track."

"What happens if Sage recognizes me?" Francis frowned. "How do I explain my disappearance from the company? When Andrea changed the timeline—"

"Yes, the timeline. You don't work for Mueller Enterprises; you'll now work for another company. Your job will be to get close to her and save her from herself."

"Can't Greg do that? He's her husband." Francis shook his head. "This won't work. I know it won't."

"Frank, this is your specialty." Leonardo reached behind him and picked up a file. "Here, read this, refresh your memory about the current timeline, and good luck."

Taking the file, Francis returned to his office and tossed it on his desk. When Andrea had entered his life, Paige had been working as a paralegal in a prestigious law firm, and had married Greg Stanton, a tax attorney two floors down.

I doubt much has changed. Frank rubbed his jaw for a few seconds, then sat down and opened the file. Gasping, he read about how a chance meeting caused her to give up her job and go to work in the fashion industry, gaining accomplishments in costume design, which led to several Tony award nominations, and even a couple of wins. Paige was still married to Greg, but after her sister's death, her grief manifested itself in reckless behavior. Both Greg and her twin brother Sage were worried about her, but unable to convince her to slow down.

Oh Paige….is this a mid-life crisis, or are you really grieving? Francis stood up and went to Handel's Hall after making sure it wasn't in use.

He scrolled through her life, called up Andrea's funeral, and watched Paige deliver a beautiful eulogy for her sister and brother-in-law. She smiled and laughed at the luncheon, but in the quiet hours after her children left, and Greg was on a conference call, Paige fell apart. She shut herself in the bedroom and sobbed for hours, falling asleep shortly before Greg arrived. He had tried several times to rouse her but gave up and threw a quilt over her.

For three days, Paige alternately sobbed and slept, then began to go through her days in a numb, mechanical way. Greg took her to a doctor, who prescribed anti-depressants, but Paige no longer smiled. All the joy seemed to be sucked out of her.

On the first anniversary of her sister's death, Paige raided her husband's liquor cabinet and drank everything, resulting in a trip to the ER to have her stomach pumped. After two weeks in the hospital, Paige seemed to be better, but when her director suggested she take a step back and accept help, she flew into a rage and quit on the spot.

"Oh Paige…" Francis paused the recording and sighed. "You took it the wrong way, sweetie." He fast-forwarded to the next morning when Paige showed up for work, claiming no knowledge of the previous day's tantrum and did everything she could think of to save her job.

Stumbling from the theater and weeping, she snorted her first line of cocaine from a sympathetic dealer. When she made it home, she attacked her home office and designed an entire cast of Elizabethan costumes. Francis watched in dismay as the cocaine habit grew, especially when calls to every producer and director in her contact list went unreturned. Word had spread about her erratic behavior, and she accidentally snorted cocaine laced with Fentanyl. If her son hadn't stopped by and found her, Paige would have died. She completed another stint in rehab and was currently on house arrest for refusing to name her dealer.

Shaking his head, Francis walked back to his office and sat down.

"Did her history shock you?" Leonardo knocked on the open door, then leaned against the frame. "You've got your hands full."

"Do I go in as a sympathetic counselor, the hard-nosed, no-nonsense counselor, or as part of the staff again?" Francis wondered, rubbing his upper lip with his index finger. "Or do I play Guardian Angel?"

"It's your call. Michael has given you carte blanche, only you can*not* interfere with the timeline. One time-traveling member of the family is enough."

"She's had it with therapists, and her friends have all drifted away. Where's Sage?"

"She's not listening to him either, after putting her through rehab the first time."

"True. I guess I could always pull a Clarence." He referred to the movie where Clarence the angel helped Jimmy Stewart.

"A what?" Leonardo looked confused.

"Never mind." An idea was forming in Francis' brain. "I think I know how to help her."

Chapter One

"Just leave me alone." Paige rolled over and pulled the covers over her head.

"There's a guy downstairs who insists on speaking to you. Says his name is Frank." Her husband cleared his voice and said, "Frank Gillespi. Says he was a friend of Andrea's."

"Then he would have been at her funeral. I remember no such person."

"He says he's been traveling and only heard about her passing last week." The bed dipped as Greg sat beside her. "Please, Paige? He seems like a nice guy."

Paige tossed the blankets aside, nearly hitting her husband in the nose, and sat up. "Oh, all right." Annoyed by the request, she couldn't help the petulant tone. "I suppose you want me to get dressed too." She faced him and moved toward the end of the bed. "Or are my Winnie-the-Pooh PJ pants not dignified enough?"

Greg shook his head. "At least put on a robe? That T-shirt is nearly transparent."

Paige grabbed a tissue and blew her nose, then shoved her arms through her faded blue terrycloth robe but didn't tie it. "Is this good enough? I'm on house detention, damn it." She wiggled her left foot, the heavy ankle bracelet prominent.

Taking his wife's arm, Greg led her downstairs.
An elderly man wearing a blue suit stood there. "Hi Paige, I'm Frank Gillespi, one of Andrea's former personal assistants." He extended his hand.

Paige ignored it and sniffed, leading the way to the sofa. Frank took the wing-backed chair to her left.

Looking at Frank, Greg spoke up, "You were saying you just now found out about Andrea's death?"

"Yes. If you don't mind, I'd like to speak to Paige in private." Frank smiled and removed a sheaf of papers from inside his suit jacket.

Greg glanced at his wife, who nodded. "I'll leave you two alone then. I have some work to do in my study."

*****

Frank waited until Greg left the room, then stuffed the papers back in his jacket pocket. Turning back to Paige, he said, "Please accept my sincere condolences. If it's any consolation, I know she and Tony are in a good place and are very happy together."

"How can you say that?" Paige looked shocked. "I overheard the preacher at her funeral say he hardly knew either of them. If they didn't attend regularly, how do we know they were saved? I've heard others say it also. If you're a non-believer, then you don't go to Heaven. I even joined a church and tried to get Greg and the kids to go with me, but it caused such a fight, I gave—up." Her voice caught on the last word, and she dabbed her eyes with her sleeve.

Frank's lips twitched. "You believe Andrea's in Hell? Drinking and doing drugs…you're doing what you can to make sure you end up in the same place?

Paige glared at him. "No, of course not. What sane person tries to kill themselves?" Her eyes narrowed at him. "How did you know about the drugs? We made sure to keep it out of the papers."

"Because I'm a Guardian. I was with your sister during her final years." Frank ignored the fact Andrea had died twice. "I've been sent because it's not your time yet."

Paige blinked and tried to speak, but only sputtered. Then her face grew red. "Oh, that's rich. I've had many interventions this past year, but this one's

priceless. You're my Guardian Angel? Well, you've done a hell of a job, buddy. Where were you when I developed hearing issues? Where were you when I cried myself to

sleep because my prom date canceled on me, and I nearly had to take my cousin?"

"I'm not an angel, I'm what they call a Guardian," Frank stated in a calm voice. "I understand your grief and if I may, you showed great courage by asking Sage's friend to take you to the dance."

"I wasn't about to miss it," Paige muttered.

"As for my duties, I'm not allowed to interfere, unless it affects your life. I see you trapped in a downhill spiral and we decided it was time to intervene."

"Is this where you tell me how my life has been so wonderful, no one can get along without me?" Paige snorted. "Believe me, I've never wished I'd never been born."

"That's a relief." Frank smiled. "You've made a successful career in the theater."

"I *had* a successful career," she corrected him. "Now, that upstart Madison Cahill not only has it, but I'm apparently blacklisted all over town." Paige dabbed at her eyes.

"Unfortunately, the choices we make have a way of coming back to haunt us."

She glared at him. "I thought you were supposed to have all the answers."

Frank spread his hands out. "Not always. I'm trying to figure out how to get your life back on track, much like your family has tried. I guess the question is, are you ready to figure it all out?"

Emotions played across her face as she sniffed and played with the frayed cuff of her robe. "I don't know how to explain it."

Frank waited. The only sound in the room was the ticking of the grandfather clock in the corner.

Finally, Paige spoke up, "I guess when Andi died, I went a little crazy." She swallowed and dropped her head.

Her use of Andrea's hated nickname made his ears perk up, and he sent a mental note to Leonardo. Frank waved his hand and produced a box of tissues. Rising, he seated himself beside her and pressed several into her hand. "Don't hold it in; let it out. It's okay, you're safe."

With a sudden wail, she leaned against him and her whole body shook with sobs. Frank rubbed her back as the storm passed.

With a hiccup, she sat up straight, wiped her eyes and blew her nose several times. "That's the first time I've ever uttered those words." Her voice was thick with emotion. "She died. My sister died. She didn't just pass." Paige spat the last word in a burst of anger. "Everyone says they're sorry for her passing. As if they're just walking by." She wiped her eyes again. "Then everyone went back to their normal routines. But I couldn't. I'd bounce ideas off Andi, especially if she'd go see a play or a movie set in the same time period as ours. She'd describe the costumes, so I'd be sure to make mine more elaborate. How could I get back to normal when my sister, my partner, my muse, is *gone*?" Her voice squeaked on the final word. Taking more tissues, she scrubbed her face. With a sigh, she looked at Frank. "I'm sorry. I don't normally cry in front of people."

Frank bit his lip as *'bullshit!'* ran through his mind.

"I guess I've been stuck in one of the grief stages, though maybe I hopped around? Or maybe it's guilt, because I was mad when she refused to go see the new Lin-Manuel Miranda musical. His costume designer is amazing."

Frank nodded. "How inconvenient of Andrea to have a heart attack when you needed her."

Paige stood up. "I will not be insulted in my own house. Good day." Her tone chilly, she started for the door.

"Paige…part of the solution is to stop running away." Frank kept his voice mild. "If you were truly honest with yourself, you'd see that grief is a process. You don't just go through the steps, boom, boom, boom. Sometimes it takes years to get to acceptance of a loved one's passing. Part of my role as a Guardian is to help others process the consequences of their actions."

"I don't care. I don't need you!" Paige took a step, then recoiled as if she'd hit a wall. "What the hell?"

Frank stood up and walked over to her. "I told you I needed to speak to you alone, and it's going to take some cooperation from you."

She glared at him. "You're imprisoning me in my own living room?"

"Only because you refuse to listen to me. I'm beginning to lose my patience, Paige. Come with me."

"I thought you said I couldn't leave," she shot back.

Frank compressed his lips and grabbed her arm. "Are you ready?" Without waiting for an answer, he waved his hand and opened a portal.

"Wh-where are you taking me? The ankle bracelet—"

"—doesn't exist where we're going." Frank ignored the fear in her voice as he led her into the past.

Chapter Two

"Where-where are we?" Paige tried to catch her breath. The cold mist evaporated to reveal the hustle and bustle of a backstage area. "Is that…it is Cheryl." She whirled to face Frank. "I have nothing to say to her."

"It's okay. She can't hear you." Frank's grip on her loosened.

"What's going on? Those are my costume designs…." Paige's voice trailed off as she caught sight of herself barking orders in a high, nasal tone. "Oh my god…is that what I sound like?" She grabbed Frank's arm. "Please tell me I don't."

He nodded. "Just watch."

"Cheryl! What imbecile put that pink dress on Camille? She should be wearing the green one in Act Two. Get her out of it immediately. Thank God it's only dress rehearsal. You have to pay attention; I write those notes for a reason!" Paige watched herself in horror as she smacked her assistant in the chest with the script. "Tristan's hat is too forward on his face." She yanked it from his head and repositioned it. "Okay, once Camille is in the proper dress, let's run through it again." She bustled away, calling for Madison.

"Wait, I remember this show." Paige let go of Frank and rubbed her temples. "We had a horrible dress rehearsal, but Opening Night was a showstopper. Packed house, everyone hit their marks, reviews were glorious." She hugged her arms to her chest.

"You were at the top of your game and apologized to the cast and your staff for taking your frustrations out on them." Frank waved his hand and the scene cleared.

"My office," Paige whispered. She watched as several lavish bouquets arrived on her desk. "From the producer and director, as well as the mayor. He and his wife enjoyed the performance."

A knock at the door caused Paige to turn her head. "Ooh, it's that witch Kristen. She's the one who screwed the director for a spot in the production. If I remember correctly, this is when she demands I switch her with Madison."

"...could barely see me. Can't you switch me with Madi?"

"That's not my call. I'm costume design, not choreography."

"Then could you at least put me in a better color?"

Paige smothered a laugh and turned to Frank. "Can you imagine? Gold in a funeral scene? I heard from our lighting director that she asked him to put a spotlight on her during the closing number."

They both watched Kristen flounce out of the office, slamming the door behind her.

Frank waved his hand again and suddenly Paige saw herself at another dress rehearsal, fitting a young actress into a period costume.

"Ooh, this is when I consulted on the *Hamilton* production. It was a nice break from Kristen. Lin-Manuel wanted me to do the costumes for the movie version, but I was already sketching the designs for *One More Kiss,* which unfortunately didn't get the acclaim it deserved." Paige spotted someone hovering in the wings and turned away. "Why are we still here? Nothing exciting happens."

"Not everything I show you is exciting, but you met someone tonight who would have a big impact on your future."

"I don't know what you're talking about. Can we leave now?" Paige tamped down the rising panic.

"Paige, Paige, Paige." Frank spoke again. "Haven't I proven to you I know everything? You can't hide from me. No atter how unpleasant or shameful, you can't lie to yourself anymore." His gentle tone made her look up in surprise.

She glared at Frank. "Did it ever occur to you I might not want to remember certain details of my past? What's the purpose of dredging up unpleasant memories? I can't change it; I'm in serious trouble-I have a record, for God's sake! Why don't you just leave me alone?"

Frank grabbed her arm and snapped his finger. Obviously, his current tactic wasn't going to work.

Chapter Three

Paige sputtered and coughed. She found herself alone in a strange room, spartan in design, with only a bed, a wooden desk, and a chest of drawers.

"Frank?" she called out.

No answer.

"Thank God. Peace and quiet." Paige sank down on the bed, then stretched out full-length. Closing her eyes, she tried to drift off, but her brain kept returning to the previous place Frank had taken her, and the sight of her former drug dealer.

"I don't want to remember Lucas. If I'd never met him, my life would have been so much better." Curling into a ball, she folded her hands under the pillow and sighed. "Maybe I'd still have my job."

A knock at the door sparked annoyance.

"Who is it?" Paige opened her eyes and sat up.

Frank entered the room and pulled out the chair to the desk.

"What do you want?" She laid back down.

"Aren't you curious as to where you are?"

"It's quiet, and I thought you were gone." Paige rolled over and closed her eyes.

"You're not getting rid of me that easily. I put you here so I could consult with my supervisor."

Paige snorted. "God doesn't care about me."

"As much as you'd like to believe that, He does care. And so does my supervisor Gabriel."

"Gabriel? What happened to Michael?"

"So you do remember your angels." Paige heard the humor in his voice. "If you want to get technical, I actually work for Leonardo, who answers to Gabriel, who in turn consults with Michael. We all answer to our Lord God The Almighty."

"Whatever." Paige rolled to her back and opened her eyes again. She obviously wouldn't be getting any sleep. "Now what?"

Frank laced his fingers together. "You just came up with a brilliant solution."

"No I didn't. I just want to get some sleep."

"Yes, you did, and you've had enough sleep already. Come with me." He stood and reached for her hand.

Paige ignored it. "This is stupid. After what you just did? Just let me stay here for a while."

"Fine, we'll do it your way. I'll be right back." Frank replaced the chair next to the desk and exited the room.

He returned a few moments later, to Paige's increased annoyance, having succeeded in drifting off for a few moments. He pushed a large cheval mirror, which he placed beside the bed.

"It's backwards," she pointed out.

"For a good reason. This isn't just any mirror." Frank flipped it over.

Curious, Paige watched as Frank slipped out of the way.

"It's cloudy… does it need cleaned or dusted?"

"Just watch."

Gradually, the mist cleared, and Paige gasped when she saw herself working on the costumes for *One More Kiss*. "That looks different from what I remember… why is Chase wearing spats?"

"That's because now you're working with a clear mind. Keep watching."

"Wait-that's not the way it was. The dress rehearsal was a complete disaster, and Kristen's dress ripped halfway. Here, everything is running smoothly." Paige unfolded herself and swung her legs over the edge of the bed.

"That's what I'm trying to show you. In this timeline, you're not high on cocaine while trying to calm down with Clonodine. Watch." He nodded at the mirror.

Reviews were stellar, and the cast performed to a packed house night after night. Producers wined and dined her, directors sent her scripts.

"Mystic Valley." Paige saw herself reach for the phone and call the producer. "Shaun darling… what is this amazing fantasy you've sent me? TV series… sweetie, I work on Broadway; I don't do TV… yes, I admit the whole thing sounds amazing…

"Blue people though… it's so *Avatar*… this came first? Interesting. I guess great minds do think alike. How many books are in the series? Seven, with more yet not written? What network… streaming? You have got to be joking."

Paige watched herself flip through her calendar. "I've got the seventeenth open to meet with you and the author. Ms Cook sounds like a delightful woman. While I've got you, my assistant has been listening to the most interesting audio mystery about a psychic-oh, you do? No, nothing like *Medium* or *Ghost Whisperer.* She's got a unique gift; she touches a surface and can 'see' everyone whose ever touched it also." She chewed on the end of her pen. "Yes, she's ordered the first two books, so I'll forward them to you. See you on the seventeenth."

Back in the room, Paige turned to Frank. "I don't know any producer named Shaun."

"He was a Teen Idol in the late 1970s, and on Broadway in the 90s. Shaun Cassidy, who produced the award winning TV show on NBC?"

Paige shook her head. "I don't watch a lot of television. That's the one thing that stayed the same." She pointed toward the mirror. "In that timeline, I'm a success? With various producers on speed dial?" She gave a short laugh. "What else happens?"

"Watch." The mirror turned cloudy again, and Paige saw herself accepting the Tony award for Best Costume Design for *As You Wish.*

"Wait… I didn't design for that."

"In this timeline, you did. Keep watching."

The mirror clouded over, and Paige saw herself accepting another Tony award.

"What the hell is *Santastein*?"

"A musical written by and up and coming comic book team of Morris and Hawkins. Negotiations are underway to bring Hawkins' zombie-themed *Wizard of Oz* to the stage."

"You have got to be kidding." Paige turned to look at him. "Dorothy as a zombie? I'm getting a migraine."

"It's all the rage with the comic book collectors. Look what Marvel did for the movie industry. You're bringing Indie comic creators to the stage."

"My brother loves to read and collect those. I just never saw the appeal." Paige scrubbed her face with her hands. "I suppose *End Game The Musical* is also on the books?"

"No, but possibly *Guardians of the Galaxy*."

Paige shook her head. "This reality has its ups and downs. Is there any reality where things are normal?"

"Infinite possibilities. I'm trying to show you how successful you could have been, Paige."

"Yeah. Where I'm making superhero costumes, Give me a break."

"Okay, how about this one?" Frank waved his hand over the mirror.

"What the hell is that?" Paige screamed in horror. "I asked you to show me something normal!"

"You don't consider being a manager of a large clothing store 'normal'?" Frank looked at the vision of Future Paige scanning clothing items and folding them into a bag for a customer. "In this reality, your after-school job turned into a career. The company paid for your classes at the university, and you graduated fourth in your management class. You're on your way to being picked District Manager of the company."

"What happened to my dreams?" Paige's voice faltered.

"This Paige never met Greg. You've never married, but you're very content with your cats and playing with Sage's daughter."

"I've seen enough." She turned away. "My choices are reality; success, but designing comic book superheroes; or I've turned into the crazy cat lady."

"Let me look. Oh, here's one. Andrea's still alive; you and Greg are happy; and you're still a Tony award winning costume designer who's never taken anything stronger than Tylenol. Want to see it?"

"Andrea's alive in this one?" Hope flooded her body as she turned around. "Yes! Show me."

"Remember, this is just another timeline." Frank stepped out of the way.

"I don't care." Paige eagerly watched as the mist cleared.

She saw herself carrying a wooden tray, laden with breakfast items, into a room.

"That's Andrea's bedroom at her home on Central Park West. Why am I there?" She frowned, then gasped. "I'm her caregiver?"

"Yes. Andrea had a stroke after the death of her beloved Tony, and there was no one left to care for her. You moved in to take care of her."

"What about my career?" Paige's eyes filled with tears as she watched herself help Andrea sit up and eat. "Oh my god…this is awful. Andi wouldn't have wanted this-wait, what is she doing?"

Andrea spit the food out and with a sudden movement, tossed the tray to the floor, spattering hot coffee all over Paige's feet. Future Paige screamed and grabbed the ice bucket by the bed, tossing its contents over her legs. Present Paige jumped back in an involuntary recoil.

"I can't hear what she's saying." Paige stepped closer to the mirror.

"I muted it after the scream, because your sister's yelling at you, as much as she can speak. She's being pretty awful, and I didn't want you to remember her like that. "Frank put his hand on Paige's shoulder, his tone gentle.

"But why?"

"Because in this timeline, you were unwilling to let your sister die. She's miserable, Paige, but you won't let her go. You put up with her garbled speech and hateful actions…why do you think that ice bucket was there? She's done this more than once."

"I don't like that timeline." Paige turned away. "Find me another, where Andrea is healthy and loves me."

"One more. Try this one,"

Paige watched herself being admitted into a hospital room. Andrea's face looked tired, but she smiled, and the two sisters hugged and kissed. Paige took a seat by the hospital bed and held her sister's hand as they spoke.

"Is this after Andi's heart attack? I remember this. Put the sound back on."

Frank waved his hand.

"…promise me you'll accomplish great things, Paige. I know that woman's driving you crazy, but remember, you have the power to fire her. I don't care if the director's banging her. You have as much clout with the producer as he does, and if she's making your job harder, go tell him to intervene." Andrea's voice was faint and asked for a sip of water.

Afterward, Andrea grimaced. "That felt good on my throat, but now my stomach's upset. I don't think I have much time left, sweetie."

"Don't say that; lots of people recover from heart attacks."

"Honey, this was a major one. The doctor says I only have a small part of my heart left undamaged. You know there's no hope for a transplant at my age, and I'm ready to join Tony. I don't want to be a burden to you, or Sage, or anyone. You know I'd hate being in a nursing home. Call Hospice, and just let me go in peace. Put DIY on the television, or a DVD of one of your plays. My lawyer has a copy of the funeral arrangements."

"You already arranged your funeral?"

"After the hell I went through after Tony died? Absolutely. I had no wish to dump that on you." Andrea took a breath. "It's already paid for. What's that saying, 'live well, play hard, leave a good-looking corpse'? "She began to sing softly. *"Don't cry for me…"*

"Argentina," Paige sniffed, turning away from the mirror and swiping at the tears rolling down her face. "It was a joke we'd always say to each other after a relative passed."

"Look at the scene, Paige."

She turned around and saw herself delivering an emotional tribute, greeting friends and family afterward, and helping dispose of Andrea's belongings.

Work resumed on *As You Wish,* and again, Paige watched herself being more assertive with Christian, and again receiving the Tony Award for Best Costume Design.

"So, in this timeline, I'm not on drugs?" Paige sank down on the bed when the mirror went dark.

"No, you're not. You dealt with your grief in a positive way, instead of giving into it and trying to run from it."

"What do I do now?"

Frank pushed the mirror out of the way and pulled out the chair again to straddle it.

"What do you want to do?"

Paige looked at him in surprise. "I assume you'll take me home and I'll face the consequences of my actions. Or can I join that last timeline?" She sighed. "It looks so much better than my present one. But that's probably against the rules,"

"Oh Paige, we've broken so many rules in the past few years. What's one more?" Frank laughed.

"What are you talking about?"

"If you only knew. If only you knew."

Chapter Four

Her phone pinged.

Congratulations! Enjoying this timeline so far? F

She smiled and replied. *Much better. Thkx*

Lunch tomorrow? Same place.

Sure. See you then.

Paige looked at the calendar. Every week since she'd slipped into the new timeline, Frank would meet with her to make sure things were still going well.

"Congratulations, Paige!" Her favorite director burst into her office, then stopped short. "You haven't heard the news?"

"About what? The Tony nominations aren't until tomorrow. What's going on?" Paige looked up from the script she was reading.

The director took a seat in front of her desk. "Scuttlebutt says you scored a major deal with Miranda."

"It's still being hammered out, but nothing's final yet. Frankie Grande pitched it to me, and I thought it had potential." She leaned back. "Unless he knows something I don't."

"I see. What's it about?"

"You've heard of Comic Book Spectrum? One of the members tweeted out the idea of turning a comic book into a musical, and Frankie happens to follow them on Instagram, and long story short, *Major Marjory* is being worked into a musical."

He shook his head. "My son watches their weekly show and buys the comics they review. At least he doesn't complain about doing his chores now. Seriously? Bringing a comic book to Broadway?"

"They said *Rock of Ages* was going to tank also, and look what a blockbuster that was," Paige reminded him.

"You've got a point." He stood up. "Times are changing."

"And we've got to keep up," she called after him. *Wait until I tell Frank about the comic book coming to the stage!*

Often, she'd wonder what was going on in her old timeline, but at the same time, she was happy with her life. It had taken very little time to slip into her new life with Greg, though it had been a shock to discover they weren't married.

I'm working on him, though… I know how his mind works. He'll come around.

*****

The next day, she walked into her favorite café and slipped into her regular booth, a small one at the back. Frank soon walked in, and after placing their orders, Frank pulled out his phone.

"You said you were curious about what happened to your other timeline?" He frowned. "Are you sure you want to know?"

"Did I end up in jail? How is Greg handling it?"

Frank bit his lip. "See for yourself. Just scroll through the pictures."

Taking a sip of her mocha latte, Paige steeled herself for what she was about to see.

Herself in the courtroom.

Wearing a hideous orange jumpsuit.

Back home, with the ankle monitor.

"Are these in order?" She looked up in surprise.

"Yes. You served three months, then were released to house arrest again. You go to weekly Narcotics Anonymous meetings, and don't take anything stronger than an aspirin. Keep looking."

Paige resumed.

Lunch with her twin brother.

Meeting with her lawyer.

Reading scripts.

"I'm reading scripts again?"

"Yes, you're working from home, and Madison Cahill, who took over your job, pleaded with the producers of the new show to hire you on a consultation basis. Since you can only leave your house for three hours a week, you go into the office twice a month to see for yourself how things are going. Otherwise, you work remotely, and it's going smoothly."

"Where's Greg? I don't see any pictures of him." Paige came to the end of the file. "Frank… where's my husband?"

Frank swallowed visibly. "He couldn't take the pressure, Paige. The court visits and fees, the damage to his firm's reputation…. it broke him. He couldn't handle it. At least you were able to stay in the house, thanks to your inheritance from Andrea."

"What inheritance?"

"She left you a sizable sum, but Greg didn't tell you while you were on the drugs, for fear you'd blow it all up your nose."

She leaned back and closed her eyes, digesting the news. "It makes sense. I can see my former self doing that. But where is he?"

"Living in a small rural town up in the Finger Lakes area, He does mainly estate planning and the occasional small town court cases."

Paige's eyes filled with tears. "In this life, he's still a partner in a big firm, and happy. Is that Greg happy?" Wiping her eyes, she leaned forward again and took another sip of her coffee.

Frank pocketed his phone as the server brought the food. "He's content. He lives a quiet life, with a dog and meets friends for dinner once in a while. Word has it he's joined a Pug Rescue Group and has met a fascinating group of men and women."

"Pugs? He always did have a soft spot in his heart for little dogs, but I'm allergic, so we could never have one." Paige smiled and picked up her fork. "I'm glad he's happy."

"Are you happy?" Frank bit into his sandwich.

"Yes, yes I am. I suppose everything has worked out. You're not in trouble for doing this, are you?" She stabbed several lettuce leaves and chicken with the fork.

Frank chewed and swallowed. "Everythings's fine. We were called on the carpet, so to speak, and had to promise to never do it again. I reminded Michael that you and your sister were very unique situations, where the typical interference wasn't going to work. We've not had our wings clipped, though let's just say that mirror you saw has been destroyed."

"How much longer do we still have to meet? It's been nearly two months…not that I don't like having lunch with you every week."

"Actually, this will be the final one." Frank wiped his lips. "I can now do one of two things. Erase your memory of your former life, or let you keep it."

"Oh, I need to keep it. I want to get Greg to propose to me soon. I want a permanent relationship with my husband again."

"Fair enough." Frank nodded. "Now eat. You're staying here, and you have something to celebrate in about two hours."

"I made it?" She tried to keep her voice low.

"Shhhh...." He winked at her. "You're going places, baby."

Epilogue

"Frank, you never cease to amaze me." Leonardo sank down into the chair in Frank's office. "Multiple timelines? What was that show...*Sliders*? I think you binge-watched a few too many episodes."

"It worked, didn't it? She didn't want to pull an *It's A Wonderful Life* and see what things had been had she never been born; showing her the past, present, and future selves only made her more despondent. I was desperate, so when she wished she'd never met her drug dealer, the idea sparked." Francis closed her file and put it in the drawer. "Case closed."

"No more time-travel," they said in unison.

"No more giving Michael headaches or banning us from The Celestial Lounge on Karaoke Night." Francis scratched his head. "I hope my next assignment is more low-key. At least Sage stayed on the straight and narrow."

"He's the only normal one of the bunch. It took Andrea dying to realize what a life of self-destruction she had lived, and Paige's depression got the better of her." Leonardo shook his head. "Look at it this way. If humans behaved all the time, we'd lead fairly boring lives, so to speak."

"What did you end up doing with the mirror?" Frank reached for his water glass and took a sip.

"You know I'm not supposed to tell you." Leonardo stood up. "No one is supposed to even know it exists. Rowling came close with the one she had in the Harry Potter books."

"Yes, well, it solved Paige's problem."

A chime sounded. Francis and Leonardo looked at each other.

"Wonder who's just arrived now?

They wandered out into the hall and hadn't gone far when Gabriel appeared. "There you both are. I need you to come with me."

"Another special case?" Francis grumbled. "I think I deserve some R-n-R after my last assignment."

"It's because of your last assignment I need you both. Come on."

They followed him upstairs to Michael's office, where they encountered a bright light. All three knelt reverently.

"Lord? To what do we owe this unexpected visit?" Gabriel asked.

"Rise, my guardians," came a deep, kind voice. The light dimmed to normal, and God Himself stood there, a balding man in a white suit. "Sit down."

Francis obeyed and noticed Michael standing in the corner.

God took a seat at Michael's desk and steepled his hands. "When I received my quarterly report from Michael, I was astounded to learn of some shenanigans going on. Time travel? Two humans appearing up here at the same time? People jumping timelines?"

"I can explain—" Leonardo began.

"No, it was my fault." Francis took a deep breath. "With all due respect, my Lord, it was the only way I could save my charge, or even get her to listen to me."

"I don't see an issue with showing her different options, Frank. But allowing her to actually jump a timeline… that's just not supposed to happen. What did you do to the charge who was in the other timeline?"

"I switched them, and gave Paige's memories to her, so there wouldn't be any questions." Francis' voice faltered, "I kept tabs on both for two months, before releasing her. It should have been enough time."

"You forgot to factor in one small detail, though. Twins share a unique bond."

"Well, yes, but with the timelines so close in detail…"

God shook his head. "You underestimated Sage. Look." He waved his hand and a portal opened.

Half afraid to look, Francis forced himself to gaze upon the sight of Sage, consulting a psychic.

Francis breathed a sigh of relief. "Humans do that all the time. It doesn't mean anything."

"Listen."

"You're the fifth medium I've gone to that's told me the same thing. I've gotten three fortune cookies with the same message…tell me what it means!" Sage slammed his palms down on the table. *"'Things are not always what they seem'….'Dig deeper into the sands of time'….'A page will turn and you will know.'* What does it mean?" Sage shoved his hands through his hair. "My sister's name is Paige… or is it referring to a book? Career change? There's no sand or even hourglass in our house, so I'm going crazy, seeing those three phrases over and over. I open a book and it's written there. I took the kids out to eat and it came out of one of those play fortune machines. Becky and I went to dinner, and it was on my fortune cookie three weeks in a row. Ugh." He stood up and paced the room. "It's got to mean something. Too coincidental."

"I'm sorry, Mr. Turner. I can only tell you what I see." The medium nodded her dark head. "I wish I could tell you more."

Francis opened his mouth, but nothing came out. He gulped air and sputtered. "That's-that's not good."

"You will find a way to fix this, are we clear?" God nodded his balding silver head. "You will make this right."

"Yes sir." Francis looked at Leonardo, who inclined his head.

"We will get it fixed, my Lord."

"Thank you." God stood up. "Michael, you will work with them on this. I don't care if it takes the entire staff of angels. Understood?"

"Yes Lord."

"Very well. Carry on." God left the room.

Frank, Michael, Leonardo, and Gabriel looked at each other.

"Now what do we do?" Frank asked.

Part Three:

Protecting Sage

Prologue

Sage exited the building and rested his head against the brick exterior. The medium's words echoed in his brain. *"I can only tell you what I see."*

There's got to be an answer somewhere! Sage smacked the wall with an open palm, then unlocked his truck and drove home.

After an absent-minded meal with his family, he escaped to the quiet calm of his home office and opened his laptop.

"Sage." His wife Becky knocked on the door as she entered. "Are you okay? You barely uttered two words at dinner. Sasha thinks you're mad at her, and Bailey's in tears because you blew him off when he asked you about his project."

"I'm sorry Bex." Sage leaned back in his chair and scrubbed his face with his hands. "There's just something wrong and I can't figure it out."

"Something wrong with what?" Becky moved closer and rested a hand on her husband's shoulder. "Is this a twin thing again?"

He reached up to cover her hand with his. "I can't explain it. She says she's fine, and nothing's going on. I don't know if it was the drugs that interfered with our ESP, or the trauma of being jailed…" his voice trailed off. "But you saw it, Becky. Who gets the same stupid fortune saying three weeks in a row?"

"I have to admit, we've eaten a lot of take-out Chinese, and I've never seen the same one twice."

"Glitch at the factory, maybe." Sage kissed his wife's hand and looked up. "I'll be okay and will apologize to the kids as soon as I'm done in here."

"Okay." Becky squeezed his shoulder, then exited the room.

Sage turned his attention to the screen and brought up the list of psychics in the area and clicked the link to the next one. He noted the address on his phone and resolved to call the next day.

*****

Walking into the musty bookstore took Sage back to his grandfather's den. The comforting smell of books, cigars, and old leather reminded him of happy hours playing the ancient Nintendo machine and mastering the art of Tetris, the only game his grandfather would play with him.

The bookstore not only held the same musty scent, but the soothing tones of classical music filled the air. Various crystals hung from a jewelry display on the counter.

"May I help you?" A pretty brunette looked up from her computer.

"I'm here to see Miss Wells. We have a four-thirty appointment."

She smiled and rose from her seat. "You're Mr. Turner? Hi, I'm Piper. Come on back."

He followed her into the inner office and took the seat she indicated.

"What is it you're looking for?" Piper asked.

Sage cleared his throat. "To tell you the truth, I'm not sure." Reaching into his pocket, he brought out a small leatherbound sketchbook. "This belongs to my sister. We're twins, so- "

"Your twin bond is strong, and it's telling you something's off." She took the pad from him and closed her eyes as her fingers traced the worn cover. "Things are not always what they seem. She suffered a great loss." Piper's face contorted and her voice broke. "I'm sensing a great deal of emotion. Loss, depression, anger, and emotional stress." She raised the pad to her face and sniffed it. "Your sister loved this sketchpad and used it often." Her eyes opened and she placed it on the desk. "Oh my. Give me a moment. That was intense." Rising, she went to a tiny refrigerator and took out a bottle of water. She uncapped it and drank, then replaced the cap and put the water back inside the fridge. She seated herself once more and shrugged her shoulders.

"Where was I? Oh yes. Does your sister not use it anymore? I'm sensing there are still some blank pages."

Sage blew out his breath. "Exactly. She's not touched that particular book since she snapped out of her depression. Paige used to use it all the time." Sage cocked his head. "You're the first psychic who's picked up on that."

Piper smiled. "I'm not surprised. My gifts are more unique than most."

"What else can you tell me?"

She closed her eyes. "Give me your hands."

Sage complied.

With a look of concentration, Piper's features twitched. Eyebrows rose, her lips pursed.

"I see a doorway…. a mirror…." She shuddered and let go of Sage's fingertips.

"Are you all, right?"

Her eyes opened. "I'm fine. I'm just trying to sort out all the emotions, hers from yours. Twins, you see, are sometimes psychic in their own ways. But I'm guessing yours changed, right? Ever since your sister's unfortunate incarceration?"

"Y-yes." Startled, Sage stood up. "I think you just found the answer. I don't feel that connection as strongly as we used to be. And not just because I moved across town last year." He rested his hands on the back of the chair. "It's like, even in college, we could still feel each other, and I could always sense when she needed to talk, and vice versa." He sat back down and rested his hands on the desk, fingers laced.

"I feel as if a door's been shut, but why?" Sage leaned back and rubbed his chin. "That's got to be it, but why? Would a traumatic event cause it? Because even when she was spiraling out of control with the drugs, I knew. I *knew*."

Piper shrugged. "Anything is possible." A buzzer sounded in the next room. "Our time's up for today. Would you want to schedule another session?" She pulled out an appointment book.

Sage stood up. "I'll think about it. I've got your number, so I'll call you." He held out his hand. "Thank you for your time, this has been very helpful." Picking up the sketchbook, he put it back in his pocket and pulled out his wallet. "How much do I owe you?"

"I'll take your payment up front." Piper moved around him and led him back to the counter. "It's been my pleasure. Take care now." She handed him the receipt.

Sage smiled and exited the store, then stood beside his truck, feeling a lot better than he had in days. Finally, an answer that made sense!

*****

Frank knocked on Leonardo's door.

"We have a problem." He entered and sat down. "Sage managed to find a real one, not an amateur."

"I know. We've been monitoring everything, just to be on the safe side." Leonardo laced his hands behind his head and pursed his lips. "The good thing is, she sensed Paige's protection by focusing on the sketchpad. The bad thing is, he hasn't met you yet, Frank, so technically he's alone. You're going to have to figure out a way to enter his life in order to protect him from whatever Piper's planning."

Frank thought for a moment. "I can check with Paige-this timeline Paige- and see if she senses anything different, and appeal to the other Paige, to see if she's having any issues."

"That's what got us into this mess in the first place." Leonardo slapped his palms on his knees. "Messing with the timelines. Should never have been done in the first place."

"Yeah, well, it was, and then Paige was so much happier having Andrea alive in hers.... we just have to deal with it." Frank's tone was sharper than he intended. "I'm sorry. But to place the blame on those with good intentions.... that's our whole purpose as guardians, to prevent our charges from making these mistakes, but when we fail, all we can do is help them through the outcome. We're just getting a dose of our own medicine, so to speak."

"You're right." Leonardo sighed. "If we can get him through this, I'll book us both into the Celestial Spa for one entire day, then go off to a private island where we don't have to deal with humans for a week."

"Sounds wonderful." Frank stood up. "I'll go deal with both Paiges, then figure out how to interact with Sage."

*****

"You did well."

"I thought you'd be interested in this one. I think he's open to suggestion." Piper worried her bottom lip. "Did you feel the protection?"

"I did, but it's on the sister, not him. Let me worry about that."

Chapter One

Sage entered his office at the mortgage company and paused. "Piper, what are you doing here?"

"My building is for sale, and the owner's giving me a chance to buy it first, before he puts it on the market." Piper's smile faded from her face as she indicated the large envelope on his desk. "Here's my financials and the details of the property. You'll find my application online."

"You didn't have to come in." Sage seated himself across from her and frowned. "One of our agents would have gotten in touch with you."

"I needed an answer now." Paige smiled. "I didn't want to wait. Is it a problem?"

"It's highly irregular, but since you're here, I'll take a look at it." Sage tapped his keyboard and located her application. "Everything looks to be in order…. this is a contract sale?"

"Yes. I had the agreement drawn up, and you can see the amount of sale, and the monthly payments." Piper pulled the papers out and shuffled through them until she found the document.

Sage glanced at it and continued looking over her application. "So far, everything looks good. I'll run it past the underwriters and if you're approved, then we'll close on it in sixty to ninety days."

"When will you know if I'm approved?"

Handing her documents back, Sage raised an eyebrow. "Won't you already know? I'll probably call you in about a week."

Piper laughed nervously. "My gift doesn't always work on me. Personal gain, and all that."

"I suppose." Sage folded his hands. "Anything else I can help you with?"

She stuffed her paperwork back into the envelope. "No, that's everything. I was hoping maybe you could fast-track it."

"Have you put down any earnest money?"

"He's letting me use the current rent as a down payment. He's been thinking of selling for the past three months, and finally decided to go ahead with it. I persuaded him to wait to make sure I was approved first."

"That's nice of him. Do you have a lot of clients, then, or just customers visiting the shop?"

"Both. I have mainly collectors looking for rare, out of print books, and they're quite expensive. Plus, the psychic community is supportive of each other." Piper stood up and moved toward the door. "I look forward to hearing from you."

Rising, Sage moved around to follow her out into the lobby. "Someone will be in touch with you soon."

"I'll be waiting." With a smile and a wave, she exited the building.

Sage watched her walk away, then with a shake of his head, went back to his office.

Eating dinner that night, Sage found it hard to concentrate. Sasha, his 5-year-old daughter, bubbled with enthusiasm as she described her dance practice for the upcoming recital. Meanwhile, Bailey sketched out a basic drawing for his Pinewood Derby car and how he wanted to be the top ranking Webelo in his scout pack. Sage tried to follow both conversations, but his mind kept turning to the disappointment in Piper's eyes when she learned she'd have to wait for her loan to be approved.

"....so can we get started this weekend?" Bailey looked up with a hopeful expression. "Jaden said his dad offered to cut out the cars. He's got this cool Shopsmith workbench. Then all we'd have to do is add the wheels, weights, and decorate it."

"Sounds good." Sage wiped his mouth and pushed his plate away. "Excellent dinner as usual, Bex. When's the recital?"

"In two weeks." Becky refilled her iced tea. "If you're finished, Sasha, it's bath time."

"Then can I watch *Moanna*?" The little girl slid off her chair.

Becky nodded, and she ran from the room. "I'll be there in a moment," she called after her. "Eat at least three green beans, Bailey, then you can be excused."

Her son made a face, then speared three beans and washed them down with the rest of his milk. "Do you think this design will work, Dad?"

Sage studied the napkin. "It's a wedge shape, aerodynamic, and basic design. I think it will do well."

"Great." The boy beaned and jumped up from his chair. "I'll tell Jaden we'll be over on Saturday."

Sage helped Becky clear the table and load the dishwasher, then went to his study.

He awakened suddenly and looked at the clock. 3 am, and Becky softly snored beside him in bed. Alarmed by the erotic dream he'd had of Piper, Sage went to the bathroom and splashed water on his face, then gripped the sink.

It's been a long time since I've dreamed about another woman…I'm happily married… I'm happily married.

He dried his face, took a deep breath, and returned to the bed.

******

At the office the next day, he found a note from the underwriters, approving Piper's loan. His heart sped up as he dialed her number and told her the good news.

"When can I come in to sign the papers?"

Her low voice sent blood rushing to his crotch. "It's unprecedented, but how about two o'clock? I have to run this past my manager. We've never had a loan approved that fast."

Piper laughed. "I happened to mention it to my uncle, who works for the city. I guess maybe he put in a good word for me?"

"I guess. See you then." Sage hung up and sighed, working to get his hormones under control.

Walking down the hall to his boss's office, he paused at the water cooler for a drink, then continued. "John, do you have a minute?"

"Sure, come on in." His boss, a tall man with salt and pepper hair, waved him in. "What can I do for you?"

"I've got a new client," Sage explained the urgency and the rapid response from the underwriters. "Is it just a slow day, or am I missing something? I've never had this fast of an approval before. It's just throwing red flags at me."

"Let me take a look. What's her name again?" John tapped his keyboard. "Ah, this explains it. Her uncle is Marc Jeffries, the president of the City Council. Girl's got connections."

"But why come here?" Sage slid into a chair and leaned forward. "She could have gone directly to a larger bank. Why pick a smaller one?"

"Maybe she liked what she saw? She's a small business owner; maybe she wants to be supportive in kind." John looked up. "At any rate, her financials check out. She's got the funds to support her payments, so I'm not seeing any issues. Good work."

Sage raked his hands through his hair. "I

normally have to work harder to get my clients approved. That they should all be this easy?"

John smiled. "You're fine. Go take her to lunch or something. Maybe she'll refer you to her friends."

The image of himself and Piper entwined in a hotel bed flickered in his brain, but he forced it away. "Maybe. Thanks." He exited the office and stopped at the water cooler again. *What is going on with me? I'm married. I love Becky!*

Chapter Two

"Sign here… and here… initial here… and one last signature." Sage tugged at his collar. Piper's skin-tight red sweater left little to the imagination, and when she leaned back to stretch, Sage felt his throat go dry.

I'm a happily married man… I'm a happily married man… He glanced at his wedding ring, but an image of Piper's mouth wrapped around his dick caused him to shake his head to clear it.

What was wrong with him? Ten years married, twelve since he'd even thought of even looking at another woman. *Maybe this is my mid-life crisis. I love Becky. I love Becky.*

Piper clapped her hands in delight, snapping Sage out of his reverie.

"Can I take you to lunch?" She looked from Sage to his boss, her soft eyes glowing. "As a thank you."

John, the mortgage sales supervisor, nodded. "I have another appointment, but Sage can join you."

Panicked, Sage tried to joke. "Don't you need to save for your first payment?"

"I have plenty in my account." She smiled. "Especially for a special occasion."

I'm trapped. Sage cleared his throat and pushed his chair away from the conference table. "Where to?"

An hour later, tucked into a quiet corner at an Italian bistro, Piper proved to be a charming lunch companion. Sage found himself drawn to her sense of humor as she described some of her more memorable clients, and some of the misconceptions of her craft.

"I've had people ask me if I named after of the TV show *Charmed*, but sadly, no. Piper is my middle name, and as soon as I turned eighteen, I had it legally changed. I mean, who in 1995 thought 'Mildred Piper' was a good name for a child? I was 'Millie' all through school and began going as 'Piper' in middle school. Mom was a Piper Laurie fan, but dad wasn't too excited. He still calls me 'Millie'." She dabbed at her lips with the napkin. "Your name is unusual also. Was your mom a hippie?"

"Not quite." Sage caught the server's eye and motioned for the check. "Remember I have a twin sister named Paige? I think my parents were trying to be cute."

"I like it. It makes you unique." The check arrived and Piper reached for it, but Sage snatched it away. "Ah, ah, ah…I said this was my treat."

"And I said you needed to save your funds for your first payment." Sage opened his wallet and produced his credit card. "I insist."

Piper sat back, a look of irritation on her pretty face. "You're one of those men who can never let a woman pay, can you?"

Sage totaled up the check and closed the red leather folder. "It's ingrained in my DNA."

Piper pursed her lips, then her features relaxed. "Then I insist you come back to the shop, so I can show you my plans for improvement."

I don't see any harm in that. I'll keep my guard up.

"Okay."

*****

Two hours later, Sage untangled himself from Piper's arms and walked naked to the tiny bathroom. He splashed cold water on his face and scowled at his reflection in the lighted mirror.

How had this happened? His guard had been up after following Piper back to the shop… had she slipped something into his coffee? The last thing he remembered was Piper talking about the new section for local authors, and the upcoming book signing with a historical fiction writer.

I don't even remember who kissed whom first. Her skin is so soft, and the things she did with her tongue; her cries in my ear… Stop it!

Sage gripped the sink and shook his head as her cries of passion echoed through his brain, and his body responded.

I've got to get out of here. Snapping off the light, Sage collected his scattered clothing, evidence they'd begun in the romance section all the way to the tiny alcove at the back.

Guilt slammed through him as he finished dressing in silence, and quietly exited the shop, wincing when the bell jangled. Unlocking his truck, he slid behind the wheel and drove two blocks before pulling over to fasten his seatbelt.

Checking his watch, he realized it was too late to return to the office. *I can explain my delay with a late appointment. Deep breaths, Sage. Deep breaths. This was a crazy, one-time thing. It will never happen again.* Momentary panic set in. *Oh god, did I wear a condom? Breathe….*

Calmer, Sage pulled back into traffic and headed home, praying he would act normal, and Becky wouldn't be suspicious.

Fortunately, when he arrived home, Becky was heading out the door with Sasha for dance practice.

"Dinner's on the stove, and Bailey's finishing up an assignment on the computer. Save me some, and we'll be home in about ninety minutes." Becky kissed him on the cheek, then hustled Sasha toward the car.

Relieved, Sage placed his briefcase in the den, then went to change into sweatpants and a clean T-shirt. Guilt racked him once more as he inspected his clothes for any tell-tale clues. No lipstick on his collar, no strange perfume clinging to his shirt, wait-the receipt in his wallet?

He plucked the scrap of paper out and was relieved to see he'd used his business expense card for the meal. He tucked it with the others, to turn into the office accountant the next day, and popped his head into Bailey's room.

"I'm home, sport. Wanna take a break and come see what your mom left for us?"

"Sure." Bailey turned toward him. "Then can you help me with my essay?"

"I can try. Let's go feed our brains." Sage led the way to the kitchen.

Bailey sighed. "Meatloaf again. Mom always makes it when Sasha has dance."

"It's easy to throw together, and your mom is a good cook." As he spoke, Sage fixed two plates with a generous squares, plus a scoop of mashed potatoes and green peas. "Come tell me about your day."

Bailey plopped down at the table with a glass of milk. "Dad, did you have a girlfriend when you were my age?"

"I think so. Her name was Anna, and we sat next to each other at lunch, and passed notes back and forth during Social Studies. Why?"

His son made a face. "There's a girl who always hangs around me and Austin, but she gets all giggly and turns red if I hit her with a ball during Dodge Ball."

"You still play that? Your Aunt Paige hated that game." Sage joined him at the table. "Does she like you or Austin?"

Scooping mashed potatoes into his mouth, Bailey's voice was muffled. "Austin says he's dating Taylor, and she's been playing Minecraft with us. Now Lindsay wants to join us."

"And you don't want her to?"

"It's not that I don't want her to, it's just I don't get why the girls can't play by themselves."

Sage stifled a laugh. "Son, you're at the age when girls are either going to do things to get your attention or act totally repulsed. It's perfectly normal to not be interested yet. You've got plenty of time to grow up."

"I don't know if I like her or not."

"Okay, what's your essay about?" Sage changed the subject.

"We're talking about animals, and I chose the cheetah to do my report on. I'm almost done."

After they finished eating, they returned upstairs, and Sage offered some gentle suggestions to improve the boy's report.

By the time Becky and Sasha arrived home, Sage was getting an education on the world his son and his friends had created.

"It's incredible. They have castles, and farms, and boats… it's just so… so…" Sage finished brushing his teeth, then joined his wife in bed.

"It's their generation's version of Leggos." Becky yawned and shut off the light. "You're coming to Sasha's recital tomorrow, right?"

"Wouldn't miss it." Sage rolled on his side and tried to go to sleep, but images of the afternoon flashed through his head. Squeezing his eyes shut, he tried to banish the memory of Piper's naked body to the back of his mind.

*****

"Oh Sage...." Rafe shook his head. "Fell for one of the oldest tricks in the book."

"At least that won't count against him. She drugged him." Frank paced the floor.

"Yes, but if he confronts her about his memory loss, and gives into temptation..."

"Maybe he'll fight it."

"Should we keep an eye on her?" Frank stopped beside the monitor. "I've got a bad feeling about this. I don't even know how to fix this. Paige in the other timeline doesn't have any twin issues. It's just this one."

"Let's see if he consults with another medium. Maybe you can take her place and explain the switch?"

"That's a thought. I've never tried to be a fortune teller before."

Chapter Three

Several days passed. Sage focused on his work, and soon he was asked to be a speaker at an event for small business owners, on the topic of financing. He crafted his speech with care, outlining the various loans his company offered, and the various ways to keep their accounts in order. The day of the luncheon, he was startled to learn Piper and a few other business owners would also be speaking.
Too late to back out, Sage gathered his courage as he was led to his table.

He greeted other business associates, and when he came face to face with Piper, he tried to keep his emotions in check, when all he wanted to do was drag her outside and demand answers. His normally cool side prevailed, and he was happy when they were seated on opposite sides of the room.

"That Piper…dude, she's hot," Thad Carpenter, the president of the Rotary Club, said as he buttered a cracker.

Sage coughed and picked up his water glass. "I hadn't noticed."

"How can you not notice? She's got a nice ass."

A memory of his hands squeezing Piper's naked buttocks as she gyrated on top of him flashed through his mind, causing him to wish an open bar was available. "I guess I've been married for so long, I quit looking."

Thad shook his head. "I'll never quit looking at desirable women. Maybe you need to get out more. There's no harm in looking, even if you can't touch."

"Oh stop, Thad," Gary Stevens, whose insurance company sponsored the event, admonished him. "Don't tease Sage. It's perfectly okay to be satisfied with what you have at home."

"Thanks." Sage managed a shaky smile as he put his water glass down and unfolded his napkin.

Lunch progressed, and as soon as the plates were cleared away, Marc Jeffries, president of the City Council, opened the meeting and invited Piper to come up and talk about her business.

As she spoke, her eyes briefly caught Sage's, and it took every effort for him to concentrate on his own pending speech. The lights behind the podium caught the subtle sequins on her green sweater, and his palms grew damp whenever Piper turned, and a glimpse of her cleavage showed.

I remember how well her breasts fit in my hands, and the softness of her skin…

Sage brought himself back to the present with a jolt, and forced himself to focus on an older, frumpy-looking woman who owned the knitting shop. Thankfully, his body settled down too. He clapped with the others when Piper's talk concluded and was thankful when the knitting lady was introduced.

Thad nudged him. "You didn't tell me you knew Piper."

"I didn't think it was necessary. Why?"

"I'd love you to introduce her to me. She said she's expanding; maybe my brother can help her out with her lumber needs. He owns the lumber yard on the edge of town."

"So go introduce yourself."

"Yeah, but she publicly thanked you, Sage. It would carry more clout if you did it."

Tamping down his impatience, Sage nodded, then clapped at the end of the knitting lady's speech.

"Next, I'd like to introduce Sage Turner, who's here to talk about ways to finance your projects and avoid the bookkeeping mistakes. Sage?"

Gathering his notes, Sage made his way to the podium and spoke at length, with the aid of the power point program he'd brought. He fielded questions at the end, and with a sigh, escaped back to his seat.

"That was great." Gary extended his hand across the table. "You had some excellent points."

"Thanks." Sage shook his hand, then sat down.

After one more presentation, the program concluded. At Thad's urging, Sage reluctantly made his way to Piper. "Enjoyed your talk and appreciate the shout out."

She beamed at him. "I owe it all to your bank

for allowing me this chance."

Thad elbowed him. Sage made the introductions. As soon as Thad mentioned his brother's lumber business, her eyes lit up. "I'm actually needing some custom-built bookshelves."

Sage excused himself and circulated, speaking to other colleagues before making his escape back to his office.

His phone chirped, signaling a reminder. He was due at the next medium's place in an hour. Finishing up paperwork took the better part of his allotted time, then he logged off and collected his briefcase. Checking the address, he frowned. It wasn't in the best neighborhood, but it was the last one on his list.

I had a good response from Piper; do I really need to consult with another one? Who knows what this one will share, or will it be like the others, who couldn't explain anything? You'll never know if you don't go. What do you have to lose?

The internal war raged all the way to the east side of town.

If I walk in and get any weird vibes, I'll leave.

Decisive, Sage exited his truck and entered the dingy building with the peeling paint and graffiti sprayed on the adjacent business. Once inside, though, he found himself in a comic bookstore, with secondhand records and movie memorabilia.

"Can I help you?" The balding middle-aged man sporting a long white ponytail and matching goatee looked up from behind the counter.

"I'm looking for Frank Gillespi."

"You found him. Welcome, Sage. I've been expecting you."

Taken aback, Sage sputtered, "Y-you know my name?"

"Of course. You made the appointment." Frank stood up and offered his hand.

Mentally kicking himself, Sage offered a sheepish grin as he shook Frank's hand. "Yeah."

"Sorry. Couldn't resist teasing you." Frank released his hand and closed his eyes. "Oh. You're seeking answers about your twin sister." He opened them again and smiled. "Come on back and let's talk."

Sage followed him to the back of the store. "If you don't mind me asking, how much business do you get in this location?"

"You'd be surprised. Here, have a seat." Frank produced two folding chairs. "I used to have a place in an upscale neighborhood, but the kids only wanted to read, never buy. When I found this place, the local kids were thrilled. We host Magic The Gathering tournaments, and other card games. Everyone's excited about vinyl coming back, and cheaper than at Walmart. They also devour comic books and save their allowance for whatever catches their fancy."

"I see." Sage took the seat offered. "I have to admit, I had reservations about getting out of my vehicle."

"Your truck's safe around here." Frank opened

a mini fridge. "You want a soda?"

"No thanks."

"Suit yourself." Frank popped open a Mountain Dew and took a few sips as he took the seat opposite Sage. "Now then…you're seeking answers about your sister. You're getting conflicting thoughts, and she's not acting like herself. Am I getting warm?"

"Have you been talking to Piper Wells?" Shocked, Sage stood up.

"No, I haven't. I'll be honest with you, but you have to hear me out. Sit down."

Sage obeyed, but his brain churned with questions.

Frank continued, "I'm what you call a Guardian. Not angel, per se, but someone who watches over you. When I see one of my charges whose life is going off the rails, well, that's when I intervene."

Blinking, Sage tried to comprehend what he was hearing. "Wh-what? You're not clairvoyant…a medium?"

"I know it's a lot to take in. You've actually met me, though you don't remember. I was your sister Andrea's assistant in another lifetime."

Listening to Frank talk about Andrea's messed up timeline made Sage's head spin. "Wait… you're saying my sister died twice? Because of Tony?"

"Yes. Then Paige spun out of control and changed her destiny. I intervened again and—"

"Wait—what? There's more?" Agitated, Sage stood up and paced. "You're telling me my sister came back, lived most of her life all over again, and that's why everything's fucked up? What did you do to Paige?"

"Not quite. I intervened when Paige was facing significant prison time. She chose to enter a reality where Andrea was still alive. It helped relieve her depression."

"But she's here." Sage felt agitated as he clenched his hands. "I can't believe what I'm hearing."

"Would you like to see your Paige? I checked on her yesterday and she's perfectly happy. Remember those phrases? *'Dig deeper in the sands of time'....'Turn a page and you will know'....'Things aren't always what they seem'."*

"Yes, but what do they mean?" Sage returned to his seat and rubbed his hands on his knees.

"Sands of time, means there are alternate timelines, or that your timeline has been manipulated in some way. In your case, Tony changed it, then Andrea, in order to 'fix' their destinies. Paige decided she wanted to live in an alternate universe, so she swapped places with her doppelganger, in a manner of speaking. Unfortunately, that left you all by yourself, and the twin bond you shared was broken. You don't have that bond with the new Paige, so only you felt the difference. Am I making any sense?"

"I—somewhat. It's just a lot to take in."

"I understand that. Go home, hug your children, spend time with your wife, and try to stay away from Piper. We sense something dark and dangerous about her and feel it would be better if you distanced yourself."

"Believe me, there's nothing I'd like better." Getting to his feet again, Sage shook Frank's hand again and made his way through the store, halting by one of the vinyl records. "Nickelback. Becky had a crush on Chad Kroeger when she was ten. How much for this?"

Frank told him, and Sage handed over his credit card. Then Frank handed it back. Clutching the album, Sage hurried home.

*****

"Ohmygod!" Becky squealed. "I always wanted this album! Thank you so much."

"I almost got a Metallica one, but I'll go get it next week."

"Where did you find it?" Becky hugged him, then caressed the album cover.

"This little hole-in-the-wall place a client told me about." Sage slid his hand down and patted his wife's posterior. "We'll celebrate later."

She leaned into him. "Go get ready for Bailey's scout meeting. I'm going to put this in the living room."

He kissed her temple, then went to change into jeans and a clean shirt. He went to collect Bailey and headed to school.

During the meeting, his phone chimed.

Excusing himself from the group of parents, he went out into the hall and found an urgent text from Becky.

Who is Piper?

His blood ran cold.

A client. Why?

We'll talk more at home.

An uneasy feeling settled in his stomach. Why would Piper contact Becky? Unless she was trying to *Basic Instinct* on him. But surely, she wasn't that devious? Anxiety gnawing, Sage was happy when the hour-long meeting adjourned, and he sped home.

He entered the house.

"Get ready for bed, Bailey," Becky called from somewhere inside.

Sage stared at the Metallica album on the coffee table, a sticky note affixed to it. Slowly, he picked it up and read the brief note.

Thanks again! Talk soon.

Piper

His phone chimed again, this time the text was from his sister.

Yo Bro… call me crazy, but you ok? Talk to me.

It sounded like his normal Paige…

Yo Crazy… doing ok. Just stressed.

Becky entered the room. "I just finished giving Sasha her bath and told Bailey he could watch an episode of *Mythbusters* before bed." She folded her arms. "Care to explain why a strange woman would drop off a vinyl record at eight o'clock in the evening?"

"No clue." Sage held his hands up, palms outward. "I helped her get a mortgage on her shop and ran into her at the Chamber event. Introduced her to Thad Carpenter, so she could get custom bookshelves made."

"She's not the hole-in-the-wall owner?" Becky visibly relaxed.

"No. We didn't even talk about music. She's just…weird."

"Okay. Sorry for acting suspicious." Taking his hand, Becky pulled him into her arms. "It's just you've been distant for a few weeks, and then out of the blue, this happens."

"It's okay. Have you played Nickelback yet?"

Becky drew back and smiled. "Sasha was fascinated. Come on." Eyes sparkling, she laced her fingers with his and led him into the family room. Turning on the record player, she carefully placed the needle in the groove halfway. The familiar piano strains of *If Everyone Cared* filled the room. "Dance with me?"

"You bet." Sage swung her into his arms. "Didn't we dance to this at our wedding?"

"Yes. Hush." She began singing, and Sage joined in. After the song was over, Becky replaced the needle in the cradle and turned off the machine. "I'll go tuck Bailey in." She kissed him briefly and hurried off.

Sage made sure the doors were locked and the lights off, then met his wife in their bedroom.

"Now I can thank you properly." Shedding her

clothes, Becky slid naked between the sheets.

Eager, Sage followed her example and snapped off the lights as he felt her fingers curl around him. Their coupling was brief and frenzied, and afterward, Sage cradled her in his arms and fell asleep.

The incessant beeping of the alarm awakened him out of a sound sleep. Becky's hair was caught beneath his arm, and he heard a grunt of protest as she reached to shut it off.

"Morning." She rolled toward him again and slipped her tongue into his mouth.

His hands found her breasts, then slipped lower. "We haven't done this in a while."

"I know. Not even on a Saturday." Her lips nuzzled his neck as he worked a finger into her folds. "I've missed this." Throwing her leg over his hip, she drew him inside. "I love you."

"I love you." He rolled on top of her and slowed his pace.

"You're going to be late…."

"I don't care. I need to spend more time with my wife." He took a breast in his mouth and heard her moan in response, felt her nails rake his back. When she called his name, he increased the pace and found his own release. "Now that's the way to start the day." He rested his weight on his elbows and smoothed her damp hair from her forehead.

"I agree." She slid her gaze over. "Crap. I've got to get the kids up for school." He rolled off of her and she slid a hand down his chest. "It hasn't been that good between us for a while."

Propping his head in his hands, Sage watched her slide out of bed and throw on a bathrobe. "Bex? Let's not try to get in rut like our parents."

"I think becoming parents with busy children creates the rut, but we don't have to follow it." Becky winked and tied the sash of her robe, then exited the room.

Sage fell back on the pillow for a few moments, then climbed out of bed to shower and start his day.

On his lunch hour, he took the Metallica album back to Piper.

"You didn't like it?" She seemed surprised and disappointed.

"It's not that. I know you're clairvoyant, but don't use your gift on me. I finally found the answer I needed, so any other business between us is over."

She smiled. "Oh Sage. You mean what took place between us didn't mean anything?"

He winced. "It was a mistake. I've never cheated on my wife before, and don't intend to do so again."

"That's unfortunate, because I thought we were good together." Placing the album on the counter, she came around and slid her arms around his waist. "Don't you remember?"

"Piper… don't do this." Sage took her hands in his and tried to loosen her grip.

"Don't what?" She plastered her lips against his.

He felt himself weaken as one of her hands

worked its way between them and his traitorous body responded. "I can't," he groaned.

"But we're so good together…"

"Oh Christ." Giving in to the sensation, he cupped her head and let his tongue take control of her mouth.

Dimly, he was aware of movement, then clothing went flying. Her breasts in his hands, then in his mouth. His lips on her sex, then her mouth on his. Thrusts deep as he watched her eyes, dark with passion. They reversed, and his hands slid from her breasts to her slim hips as she gyrated. Sage flipped her over again and slid his tongue into her mouth as he found his release.

"Damn…." He panted. "How did we get down here? The last thing I remember is slamming you against the wall."

She sighed and nuzzled his neck. "I don't know. I don't even know if I even locked the door."

"Better go check." Sage patted her backside.

Piper groaned and rolled to her knees, then stood up and threw his shirt over her nakedness.

Sage located his boxer briefs and put them on, discarding the condom first. At least he'd had sense to put that on first, but wait—where had it come from?

Piper returned. "All locked up." Shedding his shirt, she pressed herself against him. "That was better than the first time."

"Piper, we can't keep doing this. I'm married… I don't…"

"Ssshh." She put a finger to his mouth. "I know. I don't care about your marital status. All I care about is the pleasure I bring you."

"But—"

Her kiss swallowed his protest. Piper gripped him through his underwear. "I prefer to talk to this part of you." Kneeling down, she ran her tongue around the tip of his dick, and all reason left his brain as her tongue and lips worked their magic once more.

Later, snuggled together under a blanket on her bed, Sage glanced at his phone. "Oh, shit… I'm supposed to be in a meeting in five minutes. Let me text my boss." Sitting up, he shot off a message, then answered a few more before putting away his phone. "I've been granted a reprieve, but I'm going to have to leave in a few minutes." He laid on his side to face her and propped his head on one elbow. "I guess the obvious question is, why me? You're an attractive, desirable woman…why not go after someone single?"

Piper smiled. "Simple. I like you and felt an attraction the day we met. When I see something I like, I go for it." She reached out to touch his face. "The fact you're still here speaks volumes."

He winced. "Yeah. About that. Piper, I'm flattered, really. But this can't happen again. And showing up at my house was not cool."

She stroked his chin. "Duly noted. Here's what I want. A long lunch with you at least once a week, or twice a month. Whatever you're comfortable with."

"You're incredible." He stared at her.

"I don't take no for an answer." She pecked his

lips, then in a fluid motion, slipped from the bed and stood up. "Now you know where I stand, and I know where you stand, I'm sure we can come to a mutual agreement."

"Piper—"

"Go back to work and think it over, Sage. I'm not going anywhere." She left the room and returned with an armful of clothing.

Sage climbed out of bed and dressed, mildly surprised by her attitude.

*****

Francis felt a stabbing sensation in his chest.

"Awe Sage.... again? I told you to stay away from her." He called up Sage's file and clicked in. "Oh, no."

A knock sounded on the door, and Leonardo stepped inside. "We have a serious problem."

"I know. I just saw it."

"No, it's worse than that. I'm dispatching Christopher down to watch over Becky and the kids, and Julie to keep an eye on Paige. I sense something dark and sinister on the horizon."

Francis stared at his mentor. "You think it's that bad?"

"Women don't flip a switch like that unless they're angry and in complete control of their emotions. Piper reminds me of someone. I just can't put my finger on it, but I'm sure it will come to me soon."

*****

"I admit you're making progress."

"He'll come around. They always do. He's more of a challenge, but now I know his boundaries. I just have to be patient."

"His protection has a weak spot. Did you feel it?"

"That's why you hired me. Give me another week or two, and he'll be completely yours."

Chapter Four

Sage concentrated on his work and being attentive at home. He brought in a couple of larger accounts at work, earning praise from his boss. He managed to avoid Piper for two weeks, through sheer willpower.

Becky called him one day at work. "Mom and Dad want to take the kids to Lake George, specifically The Magic Forest Amusement Park, for Spring Break. I kind of want to go too, if you don't mind."

"The entire week?"

"Well, no. I'd take them up Saturday morning and come home either Monday or Tuesday. Dad will bring them back the following Friday. You'd only be on your own for three or four days."

He grinned. "Four days without the kids? How ever will we manage?"

"I'm looking forward to sleeping in and reconnecting with my husband."

Sage chuckled. "The last time your parents took the kids, we went to one of Paige's plays and fell asleep as soon as we got home."

"I'll fix that Wolfgang Puck recipe I've been

wanting to try, and we'll go to bed early. How's that sound?"

"The one with the pork chops? My mouth's watering already. Love you." Sage clicked off.

The weekend arrived. Sage helped load the large suitcase for the kids, a smaller one for his wife, plus backpacks and Becky's toiletry kit into the Jeep Liberty. After kisses all around, he watched them drive away.

Peace. Sage rubbed his hands together and reentered the house. Grabbing a soda, he decided to finish the work he'd brought home. He'd nearly finished when Piper texted him.

Help… my store's flooded. I don't know who to call… can you help?

Shit. Sage contacted his plumber and arranged to meet him at her shop. He quickly finished his report, then logged off and drove downtown.

He found Piper moving her inventory to higher shelves.

"You have insurance that will pay to replace that stuff," he exclaimed, stopping her. "Where's the water coming from?"

"The bathroom. I tried to turn off the water, but the valve's stuck And I ran out of paper towels."

Sage sloshed his way into the tiny room and bent down in front of the sink. Sure enough, the valve refused to budge.

"Do you have a wrench?" he shouted.

"No. Oh no, someone just came in."

"It's the plumber I called. Send him back here."

Sage gritted his teeth and tried once more to turn off the water, but to no avail.

He felt a tap on his shoulder.

"Let me in there; I've got tools." Ross Underwood took the spot Sage vacated, and with an expert twist, the water slowed. "Okay, I see the problem. There's also a broken pipe. Hand me that cap, Sage."

After locating the correct size, Sage handed it to him.

"Now, we need to turn it off at the main valve." Ross stood up and wiped his hands on his coveralls. "Any idea where it might be, miss?"

"No clue."

"Sometimes they're in the basement." Ross walked toward the back.

Piper bit her lip and looked up at Sage. "I've never been down there."

"It's okay, Stay up here." Sage followed Ross to the back of the store and out to the alley. "Where's the entrance?"

Ross examined the back of the building and scratched his head. "Did I miss it?" He went back inside and looked carefully at the floor. "Oh, there it is." He flipped up a corner of the rug to show a door outlined underneath. Running his fingers around the edge, he managed, with Sage's help, to lift it up and reveal the dusty staircase.

Ross ventured down a few steps, then poked his head out. "Miss, is there a switch up there? Or a flashlight?"

Piper produced a flashlight and handed it to him. "I had no idea that was even there,"

"The previous tenants must have laid the rug over it." Ross grunted and went back down the stairs. "Ah, found it."

Sage heard banging, and a few moments later, Ross reappeared. "Got it turned off. It's a good thing you don't use the basement. Right now, it's a smelly pool. I'll have to come back later with my truck and suck the water out, if the sump pump's not working,"

"How will we know if it's not?" Piper smoothed her hair down with her hands.

"I'll give it an hour, and if the water's not gone down, then I'll bring you a new one."

Piper turned to Sage. "Will you stay here while I go get a mop?"

"Sure." He watched her leave.

*****

After determining the water level had gone down, Ross left to get his truck and returned with the squeegees and lanterns, in order to see better. Once the floors were dry, Ross shone his flashlight on the pipes. "If your friend plans on keeping this place for a time, it might be in her best interest to replace some of these ancient pipes. Iron corrodes after time, and upgrading to PVC would save her some money in the long run." He pointed out another section. "I'd say that one is also about to give way. I'll work up an estimate to let her decide. This really needs to be addressed soon, or I'll have to come back and do this all again."

"I'll let her know." Sage helped gather the lanterns and equipment to haul them back upstairs.

Piper thanked Ross, who told her he'd send her the bill.

"Is there anything else you need help with up here?" Sage looked at the rug she'd draped over several chairs.

"No, I can handle it. Is the water back on?"

"Yes, but he said you have another pipe that needs to be replaced soon."

Piper covered her eyes and Sage saw her shoulders shake. Taking her in his arms, he tried to console her. "At least we were able to get the basement cleaned up without too much trouble." Gradually, he felt her relax against him.

"I can't stay here tonight." Her voice was muffled against his chest. "I just can't."

What harm could one more night be? Becky won't be back for several days. "Come home with me. You can take a hot shower and I'll order take-out."

"I don't want to impose." She looked up at him and pulled away.

"We're adults, and you're in need. Come on." Sage took her hand and led her out of the store.

"Wait…let me pack a bag." She pulled away and returned a few moments later. Locking the door behind her, she climbed into Sage's truck. "You're sure about this?"

Sage cleared his throat. "My wife and kids are out of town for a few days."

"Oh."

Once back at Sage's house, he showed her to the guest room, then led her back to the kitchen. "What do you want for dinner tonight?"

"You." Dropping her bag on the floor, Piper rose on tiptoe to snake her arms around his neck and kiss him.

Caught off guard, he gripped her arms and broke the kiss. Pulling away, he stared into her smoldering eyes and felt his control evaporate. He roughly pulled her back into his arms and tangled his tongue with hers. Blind with lust, he unzipped, unfastened, yanked, and tore fabric in order to get his hands on her bare skin.

He swept everything off the kitchen table and laid her naked body on it, then watched her as he toed off his shoes and slowly unfastened his jeans, dropping them to his ankles. Kicking them aside, he cupped his hard shaft.

Piper leaned on her elbows and licked her lips. "Why don't you let me do the honors?"

"I will, in a bit," he panted. "But first, I want to do this." Kneeling, he parted her wet folds and slid his tongue into her channel. Lapping, he found the sensitive nub at her center and fastened his lips on it.

Piper spasmed and a rush of salt hit his tongue. He heard her scream his name, and slid a finger, then a second, inside, pumping and working her to a frenzy.

When her legs boxed his ears, then relaxed, he slowed his movements and withdrew his drenched fingers. Giving her pleasure center another loving suck, he felt her shudder.

"Ooooh my gods, Sage…I need you…"

He stood up and helped her to a sitting position. "Condoms are in the bedroom," he stated hoarsely. "But I don't think I'd last that long."

"Here." She took him into her mouth and soon her talented tongue had him releasing.

Sage sank down on top of her, bracing himself on his elbows. "That was fantastic. Now for an encore." Pushing himself up, he pulled her off the table and down the hall to the guest bedroom, stopping only to retrieve the condoms from his bedside table.

"I'm not going to disrespect my wife in that way," he told her when he saw the question in her eyes.

*****

Five hours away, Becky heard the ping of the nanny cam app on her phone, but ignored it, figuring Sage was getting something to eat.

I really should silence that app when I'm with the kids or delete it altogether. Becky turned off her phone until they arrived at Lake George, then took pictures of the kids as they hiked.

The nanny cam app showed three new videos. When Becky and her parents convinced the kids to stop for lunch, she finally opened the app to see what Sage had cooked the night before. The first video made her giggle; Sage finding the stash of cookies and pulling out a handful before walking out of the room. The second video caused her to nearly drop the phone in shock.

No—not possible!

She shut the app down and tried to calm herself from the disturbing image of her husband making love to another woman. There had to be an explanation…one of his friends, maybe?

But on the kitchen table?

Struggling to maintain her composure with her parents and children, Becky tried to block the images from her mind, and for a while, succeeded. But after the day was over, and the kids were asleep in the motel room, she went down to the bar for a drink while her parents kept an eye on the kids.

Soon her mom joined her. "Exciting day, wasn't it?"

Becky nodded. "The kids really enjoyed today. Tomorrow's the zoo, right?"

"Yes." Ordering a glass of red wine, her mother waited until the bartender set in front of her to continue, "You've been awfully quiet since lunch. Are you feeling alright?"

"I'm fine." Becky lied, not wanting to upset her.

"Rebecca Mae, I saw your face just before you

closed your phone," Marjorie Jackson gently chided and put her hand over her daughter's. "Something upset you."

Becky's throat clogged with emotion as she shook her head. "It's bad." Tears stung the back of her eyes and she tried to blink them back. "It's real bad," she whispered, and taking her White Russian, moved to a quiet corner at the far end of the room.

Marjorie followed and silently handed her several bar napkins. "Whatever it is, you can tell me. Sometimes getting it off your chest helps."

Staring vacantly out the window, Becky lifted her glass with a shaking hand. "It's Sage." The words caught in her throat, and she took a sip. Setting the glass down, she swallowed and swiped at the tears spilling down her cheeks. "He's seeing someone else."

"What? How do you know?" Her mother sounded shocked.

"I saw them—on my kitchen table." Becky's voice dropped to a whisper as she haltingly told the story of the nanny app. "I guess he forgot about it." Blowing her nose, she shook her head. "What hurts even more was it was last night. Last night! Wonder why he waited so long to bring her to the house after I left?"

"Becky, don't. There has to be an explanation."

"There is. My marriage is over."

"You don't know that—"

"Whose side are you on, Mom?" Becky threw

down her napkin. "You're supposed to be on mine."

"I am on your side. I just don't think you should jump to conclusions."

"In the off chance someone who just happens to look like my husband broke into my house and screwed a random stranger on my kitchen table? Get real, Mom."

Marjorie pursed her lips. "That was a poor choice of words. I only meant you shouldn't make any hasty decisions. I know you're upset and furious, but one should never act on a knee-jerk reaction."

"Some of my best decisions have been made split-second." Becky glared at her mother and blew her nose again. Picking up her drink, she took a large swallow. "I'll tell the kids something's come up and I can't go with them to the zoo. I'm going to go home and confront my husband."

"Becky—"

"It's a five-hour drive. I'll be fine after some sleep." Downing the rest of her White Russian, Becky returned to her hotel room.

*****

Francis knocked on Leonardo's door.

"We have a crisis. Christopher just reported—"

"I know," Leonardo interrupted, his face sober. "Remember I said Piper reminded me of someone? I checked her out; she's not human."

"Not human?" Francis sank into the nearest chair.

"A few millennia ago, some of our angelic sisters were unhappy with the way their Earthly descendants were being treated and chose to leave the comforts of the Heavenly Realm. Piper is a direct descendant of one of the sisters who fell under the spell of Lyciveous, who sparked an uprising in the demon world. They wanted to create a hybrid race of angels and demons in order to better carry out Luciver's Plan, and thwart the teachings of Christ. They now walk among their human counterparts, completely unaware of their power, until they either decide to be good or not-so-good." Leonardo shook his head. "We don't use the term 'evil' unless an individual truly does something horrific and has no remorse. Their demonic form takes over at that point and Michael or Gabriel are tasked to handle them. Unless, of course, another Dark One gets to them, or other intervention."

"Other intervention?" Francis frowned. "What do you mean?"

Leonardo pinched the bridge of his nose. "Over time, spiritual people have successfully dealt with them. Priests, shamans, sensitive humans who have studied the cleansing arts."

"Ahhh, I know what you're talking about." Francis nodded. "What's our next move?"

"Becky's got a five-hour drive tomorrow, so she'll either calm down or her rage will fuel. Christopher's still with her, sending all the calm, positive waves her way. All we can do now is watch and wait."

*****

"Well done. Everything is now in place."

"I had to resort to drastic measures, but it's not over yet."

"You've got her attention, and that's what counts. It's been our experience when presented with concrete evidence, the foundation of trust is broken forever."

"What do I need to do now?"

"Lay low. Your part is over, and you will soon receive your reward."

Chapter Five

Sage awoke with an urgent need to relieve himself. Opening his eyes, he blinked, realizing he was in the guest bedroom.

Piper!

Sitting up, he discovered he was alone in the room. He padded across the hall to the bathroom and emptied his bladder, then retrieved his clothes and took them to the room he shared with his wife.

Slipping into a pair of sweatpants, he made his way to the kitchen, but it too was empty. Puzzled, he measured the coffee and poured water into the machine, then switched it on. He found his phone on the kitchen island and opened it up to a flood of texts from Becky.

How could you do this to me?

I'm coming home to talk to you. BE THERE!

Why, Sage, WHY?

How long has this been going on?

What am I going to tell the kids?

He scrolled down to see the final one, panic rising in his chest.

Disregard the above; we'll talk more when I get

home. Don't call me.

Thoroughly confused, Sage looked at the time stamp. Six am. Glancing at the clock, he noted he had three hours until she arrived home.

How did she find out? I can't believe this….

Wracked with guilt, Sage paced the kitchen until the coffee brewed, then poured himself a cup. How had Becky found out while on vacation? Had Piper called her? Sent her a picture of the two of them in bed after he'd fallen asleep?

Maybe I could claim I was drugged. She does seem to have that effect on me.

Scrolling back through the texts, he detected the stages. Shock, anger, betrayal, hurt, then calm.

All I can do is wait until she gets here. And destroy all evidence.

He gulped the rest of his coffee, wincing as the still hot liquid scalded his tongue. Leaving the cup on the counter, he rushed through a shower, then stripped the bed he'd woken up in and washed all the bedding.

While the washing machine hummed, he double-checked for any signs of Piper, even going so far as to put the used condoms in his neighbor's trash can. Sage drank another cup of coffee, this time slower, and tried to calm down.

What can I say? I'm sorry? It was a mistake…. her pipes burst and she needed a place to stay? It'll never happen again?

The washer stopped. He put the sheets in the dryer and noted the time. Little over two hours left.

Please, God.... help me to get her to calm down, to believe me? I don't know what I'd do if she leaves me. What would we tell the kids? I don't want them to turn against me for one stupid mistake.

Agitated, Sage tried to find solace in books, TV, his computer, but he found himself praying, pacing, and watching the clock. When the dryer stopped, making the bed gave him a sense of accomplishment.

Finally, he heard her car in the driveway. *God, please, put the right words in my mouth!*

Unsure whether or not to meet her at the door, he hovered by the entrance to the kitchen. "Hi Bex."

"Sage." She brushed past him and placed her keys and purse on the kitchen island.

"I left the coffee on, in case you wanted some."

"Thanks. I stopped at Starbucks for a cappuccino, but that was before I left." Becky took the mug Sage offered and poured herself a cup, with a packet of sugar and a splash of creamer from the refrigerator. After taking several sips, she reached for the decorative planter in the corner.

He waited for her to speak.

"You forgot about the Nanny Cam." Pulling out the tiny camera, Becky showed it to her husband. "Do I need to show you what was sent to my phone last night?"

Sage felt his throat go dry. "So, you saw—"

"I saw her kiss you, then you pulled away, and apparently you reconsidered. After all, I was gone for a few days. Why not?" Becky laid it on the counter and sipped her coffee. "What I want to know is, why? How long has this been going on?"

He shook his head. "Believe me, it wasn't planned. Her water pipes burst, so I went over to help her get it fixed, and she needed a place to stay. I'm so sorry for what you saw, for what happened. It was a mistake, a huge, colossal—mistake." His voice broke.

"I want to burn the kitchen table." Becky set her mug down. "Last night, I was convinced our marriage was over, and was prepared to come home and either pack up or tell you to leave. But somehow, on the drive over, it dawned on me that you haven't been acting the same since your sister passed away and Paige was arrested. The Sage I knew two years ago–hell, even two months ago–was more rational. Are you going through some sort of crisis like Paige? Do I need to take you to a psychiatrist, or a doctor? Maybe you've got a brain tumor or something."

Sage blinked, leaning against the island. "What do you mean, I'm acting irrational?"

"Ever since Paige was sentenced to House Arrest, you've been, oh, I don't know, distant. We used to all watch TV or movies at night, but you started spending more and more time in your home office, having mysterious meetings every afternoon, and then you keep running into Piper."

Clearing his throat, Sage nodded. "Part of it is the twin bond. Paige's breakdown has a little to do with it, and I've felt like I haven't t just lost one sister, but two. Then there was the odd coincidence of the fortune cookies and those silly fortunes at the fair.

I've gotten a little obsessed over the meaning of it. Piper explained it—"

"Before or after last night?" Becky interrupted and picked up her coffee again. "I'm sorry. I couldn't help it."

"She explained it the first time I met her, and now I can't seem to do anything without her popping up." Sage ran his fingers through his hair. "She used my bank to get a mortgage on her shop. She joined the local chamber. When her pipes burst, she called me. I have tried to keep my distance, but she just will not take no for an answer."

"I'm assuming you did use protection?" Becky shook her head. "Until you get tested, we're never having sex again without it."

Sage nodded. "I kept my head that much, at least."

"Good." Becky fell silent, tracing the rim of her coffee cup. "This seems so strange, to be talking about this in this way. I thought we'd be screaming at each other."

"I know. I'm relieved you aren't."

"I'm still—upset." Becky's voice broke and when she looked up, her cheeks were wet with tears. "I love you. I've never even looked at another man since I met you, and it's going to take a lot of time to earn my trust back, if ever."

"I know, and I'm so sorry."

"About getting caught, or cheating on me?" Becky swiped at her face. "Be very careful how you answer that."

Sage felt his own eyes tear up. "Becky, I've been eaten up with guilt since I met her. I'll admit I was flattered that she sought me out for advice, but she made me uncomfortable. I've tried to limit my contact with her, but she was persistent."

"I almost want to go give her a piece of my mind." Becky set her mug back down and turned back toward the door. "I left my suitcase in the car. I wasn't sure how this was going to go."

Sage rushed around her. "I'll get it. Go sit down and relax."

"I've been doing nothing but sitting. But thank you." Becky retreated.

Sage left to get her bags from the back of the minivan. Letting himself back in the house, he hesitated a moment. Normally, he would have taken them directly to the bedroom, but now….

Screw it. I'll put it on the bed and let her decide.

He found Becky drinking another mug of coffee in the living room. *Lord, give me the right words!*

"So, tell me, how did you meet Piper again?" she asked.

Sitting down in the adjacent chair, Sage sighed. "I had made a list of fortune tellers and mediums in the area and was visiting each one."

Becky blinked. "Fortune tellers? Oh, Sage… they're nothing but phonies, out to get your money."

"I was beginning to think so also, but then I walked into Piper's bookstore, and she had the only explanation that made sense, other than Frank's."

"Frank? Who's Frank?" Becky leaned forward and frowned.

Sage bit his tongue, wishing he hadn't mentioned Frank. But this called for brutal honesty, and if he wanted his wife back, now was not the time to fudge the truth.

"Frank is… I guess you could call, a guardian angel."

Becky gaped at him, then laughed. "Okay, you had me for a moment. Really, who is he?"

"I'm trying to tell you… just hear me out, please?" Sage put up his hands as she opened her mouth. "I'm serious, Bex. He told me things about Andrea and Paige…what's wrong?"

Becky's eyes had filled with tears as she shook her head back and forth. "Oh Sage. Honey--I'll call your doctor in the morning. I didn't realize what a strain you've obviously been under."

"But I'm not! I'm telling you the truth." Getting to his feet, Sage yelled at the ceiling. "Frank? Frank! Please show yourself so my wife won't think I'm crazy. Frank!"

******

Francis paced in his office, helpless as he watched Sage try to hang onto his marriage and sanity.

"I know it's killing you, but until Gabriel gives the all-clear signal, you cannot go down. Christopher has taken refuge inside the house." Leonardo mentioned their Protection Angel. "At least until all is safe, now all we can do is trust in the plan." Leonardo looked up from the monitor.

"Even though Sage feels totally abandoned?" Francis kicked a chair, sending it spinning against the wall. "I never should have revealed myself."

"Relax, Frank." Leonardo redirected his attention to the monitor when it pinged. "Okay, Gabe gave the signal. Let's go down; he and Michael are in position."

"Thank God," Francis exited the office.

*****

"Well done. I did not expect this twist, but if she gets him under a doctor's care, then this makes things easier."

"How, my lord?" Piper asked.

"He'll lose his faith entirely, as well as his family. Who knew he'd be this easy? Humans, while sometimes unpredictable are at the same time, very predictable. You just have to find the right weakness."

"Are you sure?"

"Do you doubt me?" He growled.

"N-no sire."

"Watch and wait."

Chapter Six

Two days later…

Sage stared at the solitaire hand spread out on the table, then glanced at the clock. Twelve more hours, then he could check himself out of the mental health ward of the local hospital. He'd endured psychiatric tests, personality tests, and met with a licensed therapist.

Even he was beginning to doubt his own sanity. Had the whole thing been a dream? Maybe after checking himself out, he'd go back to that last medium's office and check to see who was there.

"Sage."

A quiet voice startled him, and a man dressed in scrubs took the seat opposite him. "Frank, what are you doing in here?"

"Lower your voice. I had to sneak in here."

"I've been calling for you… I needed you the other day, and now my wife thinks I'm crazy," Sage hissed, throwing down the rest of the cards.

"I know." Frank reached down and scooped the cards into his hands. "It wasn't safe for me to come. We'll play War." He shuffled the deck, then dealt them both hands.

"What do you mean it wasn't safe? It was just me and Becky in the house. God, I think she's going to leave me." Sage shaped his cards into a pile, then flipped over his first card.

Frank tossed his card, then slid the pair toward him. He flipped his next card, and that hand went to Sage. "Remember me telling you something wasn't right? There's a darkness we can't yet identify,"

The next two pairs were Frank's, then they both turned over nines, prompting a 'war'.

Sage won with the Queen of Diamonds. "If you can't see it, then what's going to happen?"

Frank carefully looked around. "Go ahead with your plan to check out in the morning and return home. I'll talk to you both there." Standing, he handed the rest of the pack to Sage. "Just try to be patient. And Sage? Keep praying. This battle is for your soul." He patted Sage on the shoulder. "I'll be in touch."

Sage caught his hand. "H-how did you know what I was planning to do?" He blinked in surprise.

"Because it's what I would do. I'll see you tomorrow." Frank squeezed his shoulder and left the room.

*****

The next day, against everyone's protests, Sage dressed and signed himself out.

Becky picked him up, but she wasn't happy.

"Sage, do you think this is wise?"

"I'll explain once we're at the house. Just take me home." Sage fastened his seat belt and listened to the radio during the drive.

Entering the house, he stared in disbelief at the piles of items in the living room. "Are you leaving me? Or throwing me out?"

Becky pursed her lips and crossed her arms. "I haven't decided yet. On one hand, I don't ever want to set foot in the dining room or our bedroom, but on the other hand, the kids love this house. So I'm torn."

"But I can explain!"

"Explain what?" Becky put her hands on her hips. "That you talk to angels, you consult fortune tellers. And brought one home while the kids and I were gone, and it's all due to your so-called Twin Bond, which you no longer feel toward a sister you've not spoken to in months."

"Paige and I used to text each other weekly and sometimes daily, but she's been distant the past month or so. And then those stupid messages kept popping up…I was desperate for answers, Becky."

"So, you keep saying. That's why I question your sanity, Sage! I can't have a husband who can't face reality." Tears streaked down her face. "I have to think of the kids." Her voice dropped to a whisper.

A knock at the door sent Becky into the kitchen. "You deal with whomever it is while I get myself back under control."

Shaking his head, Sage went to the door, then

opened it to admit Frank and two others. "Boy, am I ever glad to see you," he exclaimed.

The three men entered, and Frank introduced his colleagues. "This is Christopher, and the other is Leonardo." Christopher stayed near the door, while Sage ushered Leonardo and Frank into the living room.

"Forgive the mess…. Becky? We're ready for you." Sage went to the kitchen, where he found his wife looking in the refrigerator. "What are you doing?"

"Trying to decide if I want to fix dinner or go out to eat."

"Frank and Leo want to talk to you."

She slammed the refrigerator door so hard the bug spray canister on top fell over. "Enough of your delusions!" she shouted. "Don't draw me into that nonsense."

"But it's not—"

"It's okay, Sage." Frank appeared in the doorway. "Becky, I know you're upset and angry with your husband, and you feel betrayed and confused. I promise you, if you come into the living room, all your questions will be answered. Please trust me?"

Becky chewed at her bottom lip. "This is Frank? He doesn't look very angelic."

"Does this?" Christopher materialized next to him.

Becky stumbled backwards against the counter. "You! I kept seeing you all over Lake

George!"

"Yes, it was Christopher's job to watch over you and the kids," Frank said. "Return to your post, Chris." A look passed between the two men.

Christopher turned and left the room.

"Sage, what the hell just happened?" Becky inched further away.

"I told you; Frank is real. I didn't know anything about Christopher." Sage reached out a hand to her. "Please, sweetheart…I'm begging you to please listen to what they have to say."

"You're not crazy… I'm not dreaming—holy shit." Closing her eyes for a moment, Becky reached out and grabbed Sage's hand, then opened her eyes again and nodded.

Sage put his arm around her as they followed Frank back to the living room and moved a few piles to sit down on the couch.

Frank sat down opposite them. "Becky, I know this is a lot to take in, but I really am what they call a Guardian, tasked with looking after you and making sure things stay on track. We only intervene if things get too bad–like now for example–otherwise, we don't interfere with your free will." He looked at Leonardo, who nodded.

"But I don't understand. I've done nothing wrong." Becky twisted her hands together.

"You're right, you haven't. This entire mess began when Andrea died and one of our junior Guardians decided to take matters into his own hands." Frank recounted what happened to Andrea and Tony. "Then, Sage's sister Paige entered the picture. The first time, she was bitter towards her older sister, but the second time, they had a close, loving relationship, and when Andrea had her heart attack—"

Becky nodded. "She grieved, lost her job, and started taking drugs."

"Yes. I helped her through that and did what I thought was right at the time." Frank shook his head. "I tried other tactics with her, but ultimately, she wanted a reality where Andrea was alive, so I switched them."

Becky gasped. "Wh-what do you mean, you switched them?"

"Alternate reality, Bex. Remember watching *Sliders* on Syfy Channel? It actually exists." Sage put his hand on her knee.

"You're kidding."

"I wish I were," Frank stated. "I thought that was the end of everything, but then we noticed Sage was feeling lost. He and Paige were so close, but with her gone and another version in her place…he was missing something."

"Your Twin Bond." Becky turned to her husband and put her hand on his arm. Turning back to Frank, she cocked her head. "You're telling me this mess we're in at the moment is actually your fault?"

"In a way. If I hadn't had to resort to such drastic measures with Paige, you and Sage would have been fine. But we underestimated Piper."

"What's she got to do with everything?" Becky sounded indignant. "Other than the fact she seduced Sage and seems obsessed with him."

"She's not human." Frank looked to Leonardo for guidance.

"We did some background research on her." Leonardo perched on the arm of the loveseat. "She's part demon, part fallen angel, and unfortunately has hooked up with a nasty demon band of brothers. Remember Piper's uncle? He is 'owned' by the rogue demon Feziactus, who wants to take over the Underworld. Piper finds his victims, and starts the process of destroying their faith, lives, exploiting whatever their weaknesses are. In your case, it's your devotion to sanity, and the fact you're under our active protection. Fez, as he's commonly known as, wasn't even looking to destroy you. We think he was just seeing how far you would fall. But now, he's actively coming for you, and that's where we come in."

"What's going to happen?" Sage put his arm around his wife.

"This. You're already on the right track. Your instinct is to protect your wife and family, and Fez can't stand that. Christopher is standing guard by the door. Gabriel and Michael are monitoring Fez's movements, as well as Piper's and Fez's other minions, known as Nebu and Calei. We think another minion, CoKo, is also involved, though she's not been seen in this sector. She's been spotted over by one of the motor vehicle factories, where they're trying to build the self-driving cars. Maybe she wants to jeopardize it in some way; we don't really know. All we do know is the more you pray to God, work toward restoring your marriage, the more you'll show Feziactus he's picked the wrong couple to mess with," Leonardo spoke with conviction. "Becky, I understand the last thing you want is to be around Sage, but you've got to understand…this is what Fez and Piper want. They want to foster mistrust and conflict between you. If you don't feel, uh, 'wifely' toward him, that's okay. Just put the house back together; keep the communication going, and above all, for the next few days, keep the kids away. If Fez or Piper get a hold of them—"

"No, not my children!" Becky pulled away from Sage. "They're with my parents until the end of the week. Do you think it will be over by then?"

"I hope so," Leonardo said. "I sincerely hope so. Frank will continue to watch over the two of you; Christopher's guarding the door. I'm going to stay in contact with Gabriel and will report back as soon as I know anything. Godspeed." Leonardo disappeared.

"Wh-where did he go?" Becky demanded.

"To check in with the others," Frank answered. "Now, here's what we're going to do."

*****

Gabriel and Michael sat high at the top of the bank building, overlooking the city.

"You feel that?" Michael asked.

"Yes, he's on the move." Gabriel jumped to his feet, looking around in all directions. "Where is he going?"

"I think he's given up on his soldiers and is assessing the situation. Normally, when things don't go the way a leader hopes, he takes matters into his own hands."

Gabriel chuckled. "Much like us, eh?"

"Believe it or not, turn the theology around and we're not much different. We want our charges to be obedient, worship regularly, and spread the message." Michael shrugged. "Lucifer just wanted to do things his own way."

"It's a fact of life. You cannot have light without the dark, the yin without the yang, the good without the evil. Utopia doesn't exist while humans have free will, no matter how much they yearn for it." Michael closed his eyes. "I sense him…alert Leo."

"Will do." Gabriel tapped his communicator and relayed the message in a low voice. "Now we wait?"

"Now we wait." Michael nodded.

*****

"What's going on? Why did he return home?"

"We don't know, my lord. This wasn't expected. We thought he would remain in the hospital, the wife would divorce him, and he'd turn to Piper for comfort. That's what the others did."

"Clearly, we've underestimated him. Let me take a look."

Chapter Seven

"Halt; this is hallowed ground. You may not enter." Christopher materialized on the porch of Sage and Becky's house.

The mid-level demon Feziactus snarled as he tried to step across the sidewalk, then winced as sparks danced off his foot. "You can't keep me from him forever, angel. You're just a lowly Protector." The black tassel swung from his octagonal head, which had brought on his name. His red, orange, and blue torso swelled over his black legs, then tapered to a three foot tail from his backside. A black cloak hung from his shoulders.

"Maybe, but you're definitely not welcome here." Frank stepped outside the door. "Sage and Becky are no longer fighting, Fez. Go look for another victim."

"They have to emerge at some point. Nebu tells me they are low on food. What are you going to do, follow them everywhere?"

Frank laughed. "A delivery service dropped off their grocery order an hour ago. Your information is unreliable, Fez. Go back to the Underworld where you belong."

"Not until I have what I've come for."

"Then you're going to be waiting a long time," Frank informed him. "Becky forgave Sage for his indiscretion."

"That's unfortunate. Does she know it wasn't the first time?"

"Actually, he confessed about an hour ago." Frank moved forward so he was halfway between the door and Fez.

"Again, unfortunate. But the groundwork has been laid. She won't trust him again."

"I know, but there's also their background," Frank went on. "They both believe in the sanctity of marriage, and the fact that poor choices, influenced by dark demons, were made. It wasn't entirely his fault."

"Going to blame us for it, are you?" A scowl twisted Fez's wrinkled face. "What about the human's free will that you all boast about?"

"There's free will and there's coercion. If a human is drugged or pressured into acting against their will, then it isn't exactly free will, is it?" Frank nodded ever so slightly.

Fez snapped his fingers.

Nebu, his flowing dark beard blowing slightly in the wind, stepped to his side.

"Try to cross the boundary," Fez ordered.

Nebu obediently stepped across but jumped back in pain.

"Damn it! Calei!" Fez shouted.

"If neither you nor Nebu can cross, what makes you think I can?" The tall, redhaired demon stayed on the opposite side of the street. "Remember, doing the same things over and over and expecting different results—"

"I've had enough of your psychobabble," Fez growled. He waved his hand and Calei disappeared in a cloud of smoke. "Never turn a psychologist. All they do is psychoanalyze every move you make."

"Maybe you should have listened to him more," Frank suggested. "You might learn something."

"I? The Great and Powerful Feziactus? Learn from a low-level deity who was easily swayed by those nasty cigar-things? Surely, you jest."

"You have overstayed your welcome and don't call me 'Shirley'" Frank stated. Gabriel and Michael, swords held high, leapt down behind Fez.

Nebu whirled around and tried to defend his master, but Gabriel easily overpowered him and struck his sword through him. Nebu disappeared into a pile of dust.

Feziactus tossed fireball after fireball. Gabriel deflected one with a sword; another one singed the tip of his wing. Fez jumped back as Michael came at him, the fireballs disappearing with a wave of Michael's hand.

Fez aimed his fireballs at the trees, but Christopher and Frank grabbed the garden hose. Frank hooked it up to the spigot and turned on the water while Christopher used it to put out the fires. He turned the hose on the demon, drenching him.

Fez shimmered out.

"Where did he go?" Gabriel asked as he and Michael stood back to back, swords raised.

Crack! The maple tree in the next yard shook as one of its large branches crashed down. Gabriel deflected it with a wave of his hand just as the car windows across the street splintered, sending shards of glass flying in all directions.

Spreading his mighty wings in protection, Michael winced as tiny needles pierced his feathers. He looked up just as metal screeched and the late model sedan took flight.

"Gabirel!" Michael dropped his sword and held up his hands. His comrade joined him and together, they managed to relocate the vehicle in an empty driveway.

Feziactus laughed with a thundering cackle. "Still think you can defeat me? Who has the advantage now?" Various yard implements rose into the air.

"Don't get cocky." Michael grabbed his sword and sliced a lawnmower as it flew toward him. A weathervane followed; Gabriel sent it back, catching Fez in the shoulder.

The demon howled and staggered backward, taking refuge behind a hedge. A flock of crows descended, squawking and attacking with their talons. They flew not only at the two angels, but at the Guardians.

"Christopher, the hose," Frank shouted. Ducking his head, he managed to turn the water back on while the other guardian aimed the water at the birds, and sprayed Frank in the process. "Gah, that's cold!" Frank shivered but he felt thankful the crows scattered. "Attempted murder, indeed. This is what he resorts to?"

Taking advantage of Fez's injury, Gabiel and Michael ran across the street.

Not giving up, Fez leapt up, the weathervane impaled through his left shoulder, but his fireballs grew weaker and he was no match against the forces of God.

"Now where's your soldiers?" Michael pointed his sword at Fez's throat. "Overconfidence has always been your downfall. Begone." He severed the tassel from the demon's head. Next, he attacked the cloak, severing the tail from his body.

Fez screamed as his features began to melt. "Not my head…not my tail! You'll regret this…." He faded away.

"Why did you do that?" Gabriel exclaimed. "You could have eradicated him."

Michael shook his head. "It is better to humiliate him before the Council. Without his tail, he's reduced back to the ranks, and will take several more decades, if not centuries, until he rises again. If I had killed him, it would have reduced me to his level, and I'm above that, thank you very much." He sheathed his sword. "Come, let us report back. Frank, you know what you need to do."

"Yes sir." Frank nodded.

*****

"What's going to happen to us?" Sage asked.

Frank sighed. "I can only think of one way to clean this mess up, and that's to send you all back to the original timeline-Paige's timeline, not Andrea's. You and Becky will be going back with full knowledge. However, I have to wipe Sasha and Bailey's memories. They're young; they'll be okay. Your mission is to keep Paige off the drugs. Get her help when you see her spiraling out of control; you'll have approximately three weeks to find a way to get through to her. You can bring up what happened, but make it seem so far-fetched you'll scare her straight. I'll be around to guide, so she'll keep her job; you'll never meet Piper; everyone will live happily ever after. Got it?"

"Got it." Sage and Becky nodded.

Epilogue

Three months later…

"And what have we learned from this, my Guardians?" God himself settled into a chair after watching Paige accept her third Tony award for Costume Design. Sage and his family were in the audience, cheering her on.

"No more time travel. It's exhausting." Frank sighed.

"Amen to that," Raphael agreed.

"You have to admit, some parts were exciting, seeing how everything played out." Christopher ducked as pillows flew his way.

"Now, all of you are ordered to the Celestial Spa. You've earned a vacation. I don't want to have to intervene anymore, do you understand?" God looked sternly at each of them in turn.

"Yes, Lord."

"I'm going to speak with Michael about his treatment of the demon. I think he was a bit lenient, though his reasoning seemed just."

"He's learned from the best, Sir."

God chuckled. "Don't you forget it."

The End

About The Author

Molly Daniels resides in the southwestern corner of Indiana with her spouse, three children, four grandchildren, and various household pets. She credits her fifth-grade student teacher for unlocking the creativity in her brain and teaching her how to write down the stories in her head. She began writing her Women's Fiction/New Adult series, The Arbor University Tales while in college, and other short stories and poetry have been featured in several anthologies.

Molly welcomes comments from her readers at the following places:

Website: **www.mollydaniels.wordpress.com**

Facebook: **www.facebook.com/mollyjdaniels**

Other Books by Molly Daniels

The Arbor University Tales

Love On The Rocks

Love Finds A Way

Forbidden Love

Balancing Act

Endless Love

Searching For Love

Love Weighs In

Second Chances

Children's:

Rex The Piddlin' Pup

Short Stories:

Night Wind (Hotel Stories)

Spirit Pottery and The Badass Fairies of the Wabash (Whispers)

Family Matters (Bad Decisions)

Rusty Bridge (Bridges)

Murder In Meeting Room Three (Mixed Bag)

High Hopes (Dreamscapes)

Finding Opal and Dream Date (Beach)

Confessions Over Cold Eggs and Tess The Skunk Whisperer (Tales From The River)

Creative Generations

Poetry:

The Sounds of Indiana (Indiana Tribute)

Milton Keynes UK
Ingram Content Group UK Ltd.
UKHW010812300424
441987UK00005B/322

9 798224 827237